Love Unlocked

LOCKED IN THE MOMENT

by Dawn Sister

Beaten Track
www.beatentrackpublishing.com

Locked in the Moment

Published 2016 by Beaten Track Publishing

ISBN: 978 1 78645 270 2

Cover Art by Russell Dixon

Beaten Track Publishing,
Burscough. Lancashire.
www.beatentrackpublishing.com

Contents

Acknowledgements

As always, I would like to thank Suki. She and I have been on quite a journey since we first started sharing our writing. I appreciate her support and I trust her opinion.

To Russ. We had such fun with those locks didn't we? ;P

To my hubby: I know you think I'm mad. I know you have no clue where all these ideas come from. I just thought I would include something in this story drawn from our life experience. Can you spot our moment, sweetie?

Chapter 1: Locked on a Bridge

W HAT IS THAT bloody noise?
It's been going on for years now. If it was just people trip-trapping over my bridge, then I wouldn't bother. I haven't bothered since that incident with the goats.

This is different, though. There's not just feet, there's wheels squeaking and engines growling and metal clanging every time someone or something wanders over my bridge. How's a troll supposed to sleep?

It wasn't always like this. I thought this bridge was a safe bet: old, a bit rickety, not well used and sitting on the outskirts of a small settlement. I didn't think I'd be disturbed that much. After the incident with the goats, I went into hibernation, and I haven't had much to do with the outside world since. I keep to myself, mostly. I only wake up every other century or so. A troll's got to eat sometime.

I woke up a couple of centuries ago to find the bridge had been rebuilt around me, and I'm now living under one of the busiest bridges in the middle of one of the busiest cities ever. Humans. They just have to keep multiplying and building bigger and noisier things.

It's not only humans, though. The bloody fairies have moved in, too. Bureaucrats and jobsworths, the lot of them. I tried to complain to them about the noise, but there was a bit of a language barrier.

I spoke to a different one every time I woke up, so complaining became a bit of a joke. Plus, I speak Troll-English and they speak Fairy-French. None of them bothered to even ask my name. Not that I care, really, because I never asked them theirs. Never mind.

I suspect I may be the only troll in France, so I don't think they really knew what to do with me. Instead of trying to find out that my name is Sol, and I just want some peace and quiet, they ignored me. That's suited me fine. Until now.

The trouble is, during my last hibernation, my bridge appears to have become the destination of choice for every bloody human that visits this city. No idea why. It was hardly used when I first came to live here; it wasn't much of a bridge back then, and the people living 'round here weren't that attached to it. Probably because of the scary troll. My space was respected back then. But since I went into extended hibernation it's become a free-for-all.

Almost everyone that comes here leaves a padlock as some sort of memento. A bloody padlock? What's that supposed to do? It's not even locking anything up. I went up to have a look, and that's what all the bloody clanging is. They couldn't leave something sensible, like a bell. That would have been nice to listen to. No, it had to be padlocks. It's driving me bloody mad, it is.

Not only have all the locks appeared, but there's also this permanent fairy guard. He's been there for at least two centuries that I can recall. No idea what he's doing, except bloody stalking me. I can't pop my head out of my door without seeing him.

What do they think I'm going to do? I know there's more humans about now. I'm always discreet. Humans tend to freak out when they see a seven-foot-tall, black hairy troll walking about in the open, so I keep to the shadows, but a bloke has to eat. No one ever sees me, except the fairy on guard, that is.

"Bonjour, Monsieur Troll." My eyes are assaulted by a mess of flaming auburn curls and pink, flushed cheeks. My fairy stalker.

He's tiny, compared to me. He's probably small by human standards as well, but I wouldn't know. I just know that he's small, annoying and perched on one of the bridge posts, grinning at me smugly. His tiny legs are crossed at the ankles while he casually eats pink-coloured ice cream with a spoon. It's the middle of the bloody night. Where did he get ice cream?

This one's pretty determined. I've seen him around before. He doesn't just sit and watch; he tries to bloody speak to me as well.

All I ever do is grunt at him, but he never seems to give up and he always sounds so bloody cheerful. Bloody fairies.

"How are you this fine evening, Monsieur?" His very blue eyes regard me with interest.

Ha! The only interest he has in me is whether or not I'm up to no good. This time, I'm up here to do something about the noise. He doesn't know that, though. Let him try and stop me.

"Is there anything I can help you with, Monsieur Troll?" He just won't give up.

"Nuffing, fanks." I grunt and then turn my back. He'll get the message.

He doesn't get the message.

"Ah, but I am forgetting my manners." He rolls his sparkling eyes that are framed by thick auburn lashes. "Allow me to introduce myself. Je m'appelle Lucien." And now he's speaking to me in French. This is going to be interesting. "Would you like some of my ice cream?"

I wish he'd make his bloody mind up about what language he's going to speak. At least he speaks decent Troll-English, but only doing it when he feels like it is a bit irritating really.

I regard his ice cream with curiosity. I haven't tasted ice cream before. I wonder what it's like. Why's he offering me some of his? What's his game? I narrow my eyes in suspicion.

"No!" I refuse abruptly, withdrawing my claws, which had reached out to take the tiny spoon he offered me.

"Okay, but it is your loss. Il est très bien." He shrugs and finishes off the tub of ice cream with an exaggerated lick of his lips. "It's very nice to finally meet you, Monsieur Troll."

He jumps down from his perch and holds out a delicate, pale hand. His fingers are slight and slender and well-manicured. Next to my long thick, hairy claws, they are almost doll-like.

I look down at his hand as if it's something completely alien. I know what he's doing, but I don't have a fucking clue why he'd want to shake hands with a hairy old bastard like me.

"Er…alrigh'?" I manage to grunt, not wanting to sound too encouraging, but not wanting to seem bad-mannered either. I don't shake the hand, though, and he tucks it away behind his back with an awkward grimace. "Look, Looshi, or whatever your name is—"

"It's Lucien," he corrects brightly.

"Whatever, fairy boy. I ain't up here for a cosy little chin wag." I sneer at him. "Nice to meet me? Don't talk such bloody bollocks. Now do me a favour and bugger off." I hook my thumb over my shoulder then turn my back again.

I'm not good with people. I've been on my own too long, and I like it that way. Usually, my noncommittal grunting is enough to scare away the mildly curious. He should be running away in disgust, but as I start to walk he is suddenly walking by my side. Bloody hell, what do I have to do?

"Monsieur Troll." Fairy Boy, what's 'is name? Lucien? Whatever, he sounds shocked, even a little hurt. "I do not think there is any need to be so prickly. After all, I was only being friendly."

His accent is as delicate as the rest of him. I could flick him away like a speck of dust. I laugh, which makes him laugh. Why the hell is he laughing? Doesn't he know I could squash him like a jelly? And why the hell is he trying to be friendly? With me? No one ever wants to be friends with a troll.

"I got business to take care of, Fairy Boy. I don't need your 'elp, and I really don't need your company. I'm sorry if you feel offended by that, but I just want to be left alone."

I don't want or need him hanging over me. I've got something to take care of. It's going to take a lot of concentration, and I can't do that with him trying his best to get under my skin.

Fairy Boy Lucien looks crestfallen, and now I feel bad. Bloody hell. He hangs his head and turns away from me, tapping at the cobbles with his toes as he takes a few steps away.

"Oh, well, if that's what you want. I shall go."

Oh, God, he's making me feel guilty now. Bloody fairies. They're all the same. Bloody divas, the lot of them. He does look extremely unhappy, though. If I had a heart, his expression would pull at its strings.

Would it hurt to delay doing something about those locks for one more night? Urgh! I can't believe I'm doing this.

"Oh, don't get all huffy and pouty on me, bloody 'ell. Come back."

Lucien turns, and his bright smile takes my breath away. I scowl. If I didn't know any better, I'd think he was smiling at me, but he isn't. He's just smiling because he got his own way.

He skips back and jumps up to perch himself nimbly on the bridge post once more. That way, he is almost at my eye level, although he would still have to stretch to look me properly in the eye. Our height difference is pretty ludicrous.

"So, tell me, Monsieur Troll—" he rubs his hands together as if he is ready to help me in any way he can "—what is it that you are doing this beautiful evening?"

I narrow my eyes. Is he here to stop me? I can't think for one minute that he's here by coincidence or voluntarily. No one would willingly approach me and try to hold a conversation.

"What is it to you, Fairy Boy?" I grunt.

Lucien widens his eyes and looks away, seeming a little awkward. "I was not trying to pry. It is none of my business, really. I was just curious."

"Damn right, it's none of your business," I blurt out. "And you know what they say about curiosity. In fact, I changed my mind. I do want you to bugger off, or you can sit there and watch, I don't fucking care, but I'm going to get on with my business, and I'd like to see you try and stop me."

Lucien's eyes widen even more, but his reply this time is a poorly veiled threat. "If you are planning to do something that is dangerous, or illegal, Monsieur Troll, then I will have no choice but to stop you."

"Oh, you and whose army, then?" I laugh out loud. "There's nothing to ya but fluff, ya little pipsqueak. Just who do you think you are?"

"I represent l'Authoritié de Fée Folklorique." He puffs out his chest and I continue to laugh at his little display. "If you are planning to do anything to endanger this bridge, then it is my duty to stop you, Monsieur Troll." He stands, his fists out in front of him in an aggressive manner. Again, I just laugh, and he bites his lip and blushes whilst holding his position.

"Look at you, actin' all tough." I guffaw. "Stand down, Fairy Boy. I ain't plannin' on damagin' one bolt of my bridge."

Lucien heaves a sigh of relief and seems assured that he won't have to follow through on his threats. He relaxes. Silly boy. He has no idea what I'm about to do. I'm sure the noise will be spectacular.

I lift my hands and begin to chant. I know one spell—the only spell I ever bothered to learn, and the only one I've ever needed. It's served me well in the past, and it's about to help me once again.

It takes a few seconds before Fairy Boy registers what I'm doing.

"Attends! Monsieur Troll. What are you doing? Spell casting is forbidden in view of humans."

"Relax. They wouldn't know a spell if it hit them in the face and turned them into a frog." I resume my chant. "There ain't any humans about, anyway."

"Mais, Monsieur Troll, you must not cast a spell here. It could damage your bridge if it is not cast properly."

"Are you doubting my spell casting skills, Fairy Boy?" I growl. "I was casting spells long before you fairy lot were even sparkling dust."

"Non, mais non, juste…s'il vous plait, Monsieur Troll. Your skills are not in question here, but the efficacy of the spell. If it is not a legitimate spell, one wrong word could blow up half of Paris."

Hmm, interesting thought.

"Don't go giving me ideas." I grin wickedly at him. He widens his eyes and gasps.

"Relax, I ain't gonna blow up Paris. I just want some peace and quiet, that's all. And this spell will help me get it."

I raise my hands again and repeat the charm that was interrupted. Lucien regards me with a frown.

"How can an opening spell possibly give you peace and quiet, Monsieur Troll?"

I ignore him as I finish the last words and cast the spell. As I do, I think Lucien realises what is about to happen. He gives a shout, jumps in front of me and screeches a counter-charm, but it's too little too late.

With a resounding, satisfying click, every single padlock on the bridge unlocks. Then, with a noise that sends a shock wave through the earth because of the weight, every lock falls to the ground at the same time. They must have heard that noise all over the city and beyond. That'll teach 'em. Let them all try and sleep through that.

I place my hands over my ears, even though the noise has already happened, and it's futile to try to protect my hearing now. Lucien is knocked off his feet by the shock wave and lands in a heap beside me.

For a moment, there is silence, then Lucien scrambles on his hands and knees to the first pile of locks with a strangled, gasping sob.

"Non, non, non, non." He shakes his head rapidly, his hands go up to pull at his hair as he stands and stares at the rest of the locks strewn across the bridge. "Non, Mon Dieu! Monsieur Troll, what have you done?"

"I've done what your lot couldn't be arsed to do when I asked, oh, about a million times, for something to be done about the bloody noise. All those locks clangin' above my bloody 'ead. It was driving me batty." I brush my hands together in satisfaction of a job well done as I survey my handiwork. "Well not anymore. I might get a good night's sleep now."

The spell worked far better than I'd thought. I haven't cast that spell in a very long time. I'm a bit rusty. I thought there'd be a few locks still in place, but there isn't one left hanging. They're all open and lying strewn across the bridge. Finally some peace. It's bliss.

Except it isn't peaceful, since Lucien is still pulling at his hair and gibbering.

"Monsieur, you should not have done this. Zut alors! We are in so much trouble now." He's all wild eyed and freaking out.

"We?" I can't help reacting to that. "And what do you mean trouble? This is *my* bridge. I claimed it centuries ago, before your lot put in an appearance. I can do what the 'ell I want on this bridge."

"Mais non." Lucien shakes his head. "You don't understand, Monsieur Troll. You have done something terrible. The whole of Paris, the entire world could be thrown into chaos because of this."

"Sounds bloody marvellous." I grin at his sheer shock and panic. "Just as long as they don't disturb me, then I don't give a rat's arse."

Lucien gives me a look of utmost horror. "Monsieur, have you no heart?"

"No!" I shout at him. "I'm a troll."

"Even trolls have hearts, Monsieur."

"Not this one." I turn in order to walk away but stop and can't help shouting out in surprise as I am confronted by a dozen fairies, all looking as filled with panic as Lucien does. All except for one: a woman, who stands a little taller than the rest and in the centre of the pack. Her long auburn hair glitters like it's made of sunsets. She's wearing a sparkling silver business suit, and her arms are folded across her chest. Her eyes are narrowed, and she has an angry scowl on her beautiful face.

"What have you done?" she practically screams at me.

I am a grumpy, bad-tempered troll, and I am not accustomed to being screamed at angrily by pipsqueak fairies, no matter how important they look. I place my claws on my hips and loom over her.

"I've done something your bloody lot should've done years ago, lady."

"Troll, I am no lady." She hisses, her eyes narrowed to slits. "I am your queen."

I raise my bushy eyebrows a little, because, if she is The Fairy Queen, then she is technically my queen too. I never really saw myself as Fairy Folk, because I'm not all that delicate and fairy-like, but trolls do fall under that category.

"Your Majesty." Lucien bows gracefully as he moves to my side. He steps forward confidently, and there is a determined set to his shoulders as he straightens up. "I can explain what happened—"

"I'll deal with you later, Lucien," the queen hisses and Lucien gasps in horror, stepping back, his confidence shaken. He steps behind me, as if using me as a shield.

Before I can react to that, the queen has turned her attention back to me, and the look on her face makes me gulp ever so slightly. I think Lucien is right. I'm in big trouble. I don't know why, though. It's just a bunch of bloody padlocks.

"Do you have any idea of the mess you have just created, Troll?"

I curl my lip. Is that all she's worried about? The mess?

"The street cleaners'll be about later. Let them clear it up." I sneer.

"That is not what I meant!" she snaps, and I bite my lip and shuffle my feet awkwardly.

I look down at Lucien, and we exchange a worried glance. I get the feeling he is on my side, because he is now standing beside me. I don't know why, though. Surely if he's in trouble for not stopping me, he would want to put as much distance between us as possible.

"Lucien, why did you not stop him?" The queen turns her attention on him, and he quivers slightly, pulling himself up to his less-than-impressive full height.

"Madame Queen, I did not know this was what he was going to do." They exchange angry glances that I don't quite know how to interpret. It's like there is an underlying private battle going on between them. The others step back, as if letting them get on with it.

Queenie looks really angry with him. She ain't gonna turn him into a toad on my watch, though.

"That's true." I nod, quickly intervening. "'E never 'ad a clue. And 'e never 'ad a chance to try and stop me. I was too quick."

I don't know why I feel the need to defend him, except I may be a lot of things, but I'm not a coward. I would never allow someone else to take the blame for something I've done.

I still don't understand what it is that has their knickers in such a twist.

"Madame." Lucien steps forwards again. "Before Monsieur Troll cast his spell, he told me…" The queen shoots him an angry glare, and he stumbles over his words. "Er, wh-what I mean is, if he had only been told what the locks meant, he might not have—"

"Silence!" the queen snaps, and Lucien steps back behind me with a gasp and an apologetic look.

"I'm sorry, Monsieur Troll. I tried. She is impossibly stubborn," he whispers. What's he apologising for? This isn't his fault.

What the hell? Is he defending me now? From what?

"How did he even manage to cast such a powerful spell without any of us knowing?" The queen now looks around at her lackeys, and they all shrug and shake their heads. She points at them all furiously.

"Madame." One of her lackeys steps forward, holding a clipboard. "There is not any indication in our files that he has any power at all."

Madame Queen glares at him, and he steps back with a gulp and a squeaked apology.

"Mark my words, when I find out how this was allowed to happen, heads will roll." Everyone, including Lucien, gives an involuntary squeak.

Madame Queen turns her attention back to me. She might be little taller than my knee when I'm crouching, but I am still intimidated. She's a powerful being, despite her diminutive size.

"Troll, do you know what chaos you have created by unlocking all these padlocks?"

"Er, no miss."

"Madame!" she corrects me. I bite my lip.

"Sorry!" I mumble, looking down at my gnarly great troll feet and shuffling them.

"I knew this was a bad idea, allowing you to remain living under this bridge. I should have had you moved on long ago, when all this started." She waves her hands over the fallen locks. "I was advised to give you a chance. You were in hibernation. You weren't causing any problems, you were minding your own business." She glares at Lucien as she says all of this. No idea why.

"Damn right, I was minding my own, until those bloody locks started appearing, then I tried to ask for—"

"Silence!" she shouts again, and I stop. "I will zip your mouth shut if you speak out of turn again."

Bloody hell! I shut my mouth with a snap.

"These are not just padlocks, Troll," The queen explains, slowly, as if she's talking to a child. I'm fucking centuries older than she is, for fuck's sake. I keep my trap shut, though, and let her continue. "They are love locks."

"You what?" I frown. "What the 'ell are love locks?"

"I warned you!" The queen waves her hand. A bolt of light shoots from her finger.

"Madame!" Lucien cries out in shock as he jumps in front of me.

He is thrown back against my legs as the bolt of light hits his chest. I catch him and keep him on his feet. He looks up at me, and his wide blue eyes are filled with pain. I just gape. His lips have been replaced by zippers, and they are firmly zipped closed.

"Oh my gawd!" That can't be pleasant at all. He stopped the spell from hitting me. "What the 'ell did you do that for?" Lucien gives a helpless shrug and tries to smile but holds the side of his mouth with a groan.

I glare at Madame Queen. Queen or no queen, she can just bloody well undo that spell.

"Turn 'im back, you bloody bully."

The crowd of bureaucratic fairies gives a collective gasp, but another bolt of light, a much gentler one this time, touches Lucien's mouth, and his lips part, the zippers gone.

He places his hand over his mouth as he takes some deep breaths. I steady him.

"Alrigh'?" I ask. He nods, his eyes full of steel and determination now. He glares at Madame Queen as he rubs his jaw. He still does not leave my side.

"Before I was so rudely interrupted—" Madame Queen glares back at Lucien. To my surprise, she looks away first, a flash of chagrin in her eyes. "I was explaining that these were love locks. People come from far and wide to seal their love bond within a lock and hang it on this bridge."

"*My* bridge!" I scowl. "Why the 'ell would they choose my bridge?" Madame Queen narrows her eyes but does not comment on my interruption.

"This is LoveLock Bridge," she explains. "You have undone all of those bonds. Couples everywhere will find themselves torn apart, because their love is no longer sealed within the magic of these locks. How you ever managed to unlock every single one of them, I will never know. Trolls possess magic deeper than any of us understand. No matter."

She waves her hand, and I flinch ever so slightly. Lucien twitches, as if he's about to pull the same trick as before. Madame Queen was not casting a spell, though, thankfully.

"You must undo your spell." She regards me with raised eyebrows, tapping her foot impatiently, her arms folded once more over her chest.

"I don't know 'ow," I tell her. "I've never 'ad any proper trainin'. No one bovvered to try. I only know that one spell. I've only ever needed to open things. Closing things was never a consideration."

"I did not mean by counter-spell, troll. It is not simply a case of replacing the locks. You must do it the hard way."

The hard way? That sounds too much like hard work.

"And what if I don't want to?" I ask, because what do I care about a few broken human relationships?

"I will make you want to, Monsieur Troll." Madame Queen waves her hand again, and this time she is too quick for Lucien. The last thing I hear is his strangled cry of protest as her bolt of light hits me square in the chest, and everything goes black.

Chapter 2: Locked in a Spell

I OPEN MY EYES to find Lucien the Fairy staring down at me. Staring down at me? The guy is fucking five foot if he's an inch. How the hell is he staring down at me?

Then I realise I am lying on my back, on my bridge.

"What the hell?" I try to sit up, but Lucien's hand on my shoulder gently urges me to remain where I am.

"Take it easy there, Monsieur Troll. One does not recover so quickly from one of Madame Queen's spells. Give yourself some time and sit first."

I do, holding my head and groaning as I bend my knees up to my chest. My entire body is stiff and sore, like I've run a marathon, and the world seems to be spinning a little too fast.

"What the hell hit me?"

"Madame Queen hit you," Lucien explains unhappily.

I sort of remember a couple of bright flashes. I also remember Lucien jumping in front of one of those flashes.

"She hit you too. You don't seem to be so badly affected." I look up at him, and he bites his rather pink bottom lip.

"That spell was not such a powerful one."

"You jumped in front of me, took a hit for me? Why?" I'm curious as to why he seems to be acting as my unofficial protector. I never asked for one.

"She can be a bully sometimes, Madame Queen," he explains. He looks away. I think he's blushing. Probably because he's calling his queen names.

"Too right she's a bully. She zipped your lips shut and bloody knocked me out? What did she hit me with anyway?" I frown, since I don't feel any different. I just feel a little weak at the knees. She didn't turn me into a toad…I don't think.

"She hit you with a spell, Monsieur Troll." Lucien gives me a confused look. I glare at him.

"*She 'it you weezz a spell, Monsieur Troll!*" my tone drips with sarcasm. "What do you fink I am? Stupid? Of course she 'it me wiv a bloody spell. Which spell?"

"Erm…" Lucien gives me a once-over and bites his lip again.

"An 'Erm' spell?" I sneer. "I never 'eard of any 'Erm' spell. Maybe you're the one that's stupid. And 'ow come you took the first blow for me, but not the second?"

"If I knew you were going to be so damn ungrateful, I would not have even done that." Lucien turns away from me with a huff.

He's right. I am being an ungrateful, grumpy old sod. He took that blow for me, and he really didn't have to. It can't have been comfortable, having his lips zipped together like that. I certainly wouldn't have wanted it to happen to me. I doubt I would have done the same if our roles had been reversed. Mostly because trolls don't move that fast. Also because trolls are selfish bastards. Well I am, anyway. Two thousand years of living on my own has made me that way.

"Look, I'm sorry, Looshi." The words sound alien coming from my mouth, probably because I've never apologised to anyone in my life.

"It's Lucien," he corrects me but doesn't look at me.

"Sorry, Lucien. And thanks, for taking that first spell square in the chest. I doubt 'er ladyship would've reversed the spell so quickly if she'd hit me."

"Oh, I would have made sure that she had," Lucien mutters as he turns back to face me. "Apology accepted, and you are very welcome." His smile is just a little bit dazzling.

His eyes sparkle like they're made of fairy dust, which they probably are, because he's a fairy. They are also very blue and very distracting.

My heart feels kind of funny, and my claws are suddenly very clammy. No idea why. My claws never get clammy. I go to wipe them on the fur at my hips, but they only meet skin. *What the…?*

I look down at myself and screech. Lucien jumps back in fright.

"Where's all my bloody fur gone?" I shout. I hold my hands out in front of me, staring at the smooth, dark-brown skin I only normally see when I've scratched a bald patch. "And I've got five fingers instead of just four."

They're all rounded, and short, and my hands—*oh my god, I have hands, not claws. What about my face?*

My hands clumsily search my face to find more exposed skin. I have hair, but it's all on the top of my head, like a bloody…

"Holy bloody fairy crap. I'm human!" I gasp, turning my shock and anger fully on Lucien. "Your bloody queen made me bloody human." I point an accusing finger.

"She is your queen too, Monsieur Troll." Lucien narrows his eyes and places his hands on his hips. "And you are not human, you just look human. Inside you are still a troll, with the manners to match."

"Well get you, Mister La-di-da Fairy Boy. We ain't all born wiv a silver spoon in our mouths. Sorry if my troll manners are a bit rough on your delicate fairy sensibilities." I curl my lip, pulling myself to standing and wobbling slightly on my very human legs and feet.

I try to stand to my full height, but my centre of gravity is completely screwed. My balance is all off, because my toes are all stubby. I wobble a little too much and stumble. Lucien catches me, in an attempt to stop me from falling. But even stuck in this stupid human body, I am still quite a bit taller than him, and he only succeeds in breaking my fall as we end up in a heap on the pavement.

Shit. I hope I'm not hurting him. He's so small and fluffy, and I'm so big. I'm afraid I'll squash him like a fly.

He grunts and shuffles, trying to shove me away. His tiny body is vibrant and firm, and when I meet his gaze, his blue eyes are full of hell. Something sparks inside me. I have no idea what, but it feels…exciting…in a weird kind of way.

"Do you mind?" he says through gritted teeth.

As nice as this feels, I think it's time I moved.

"Alrigh', Fairy Boy, I'm moving. Don't get yerself all hot 'n' bovvered."

"Don't flatter yourself." He huffs and mutters something in French that I am pretty sure I don't need a translation for. He's angry anyway.

I roll off him and get to my feet again. My legs are wobbly for a different reason now. A reason that has taken me completely by surprise because that's never happened to me before. I feel a little breathless. I try to take some steps. He stops me with a hand on my arm.

"Wait!" He pulls himself up as well. "I'll help you."

"I don't need your bloody help, Fairy Boy. Go back to your lacy wings and glitter, and leave me alone." I swipe away his hand and take a step backwards, surreptitiously holding on to the railing of my bridge in order to steady myself before striding off towards the steps that lead down to my home beneath the arches.

My attempt at a stride is more like a stumbling wobble. If I'd ever been drunk, I'd imagine it would feel like this: bloody annoying.

Lucien calls after me with a hint of frustration in his tone. "Monsieur Troll, you were hit by a very strong spell. You should not be going anywhere alone."

"And I told you, I don't need yours, or anybody's help." What I do need is to get back under my bridge where I can lick my wounds, out of sight of his piercing blue eyes. There's no way I will let him see I'm broken, but bloody hell, what am I supposed to do now? I'm bloody human.

"Monsieur Troll." Lucien is nothing if not persistent.

He catches up with me as I reach the top of the steps, just in time to stop me tripping and stumbling down them. He's stronger than he looks as his hand wraps around my arm and pulls me back from the brink.

"Shit, Fairy Boy. I thought I was a gonner there." I lean against one of the balustrades, holding my hand to my chest. "Me bloody ticker's going ninety to the dozen."

I'm a mess. How am I going to get out of this one? His bloody queen has a lot to answer for.

"You should not wander off on your own," Lucien chides. "Not looking like this." He waves his hands up and down my very human body and looks a little uncomfortable.

A troll stuck in the body of a human. I must look pretty damn ridiculous.

I take a deep breath and glance across the river. Blimey, it's almost dawn. I must have been out of it for a good few hours. Did Lucien stay with me the entire time? Maybe I'm being a little bit ungrateful, even if I did thank him already. He didn't need to stay with me all night, and he doesn't need to stick around now, but he is. He even looks concerned. Is that concern for me? That's a bloody ridiculous thought. Who would ever be concerned for me?

"How long?" I ask into the night, but Lucien is close enough to me to know I'm really talking to him.

"Pardon, Monsieur?"

"You heard me, Fairy Boy." I turn to lean back against the rail. Why does he have to be so painfully polite all the time? "How long do I 'ave to stay like this, and what do I 'ave to do to get changed back? Your queen must have said something before she did a runner."

"Oh." Lucien mirrors my actions, leaning back against the railing with me. "Well, you have until midnight two days from now to fix one hundred of the love locks that you undid. Then Madame Queen will consider reversing the spell, if you wish it."

"If I wish it?" I stand up, thankfully feeling not so dizzy this time. "If I bloody wish it?"

Lucien looks a little intimidated and takes a few steps back. I don't know what he thinks I'll do to him.

"What makes you think I would prefer to look like this for the rest of my life, Fairy Boy? Stuffed inside this human body? I'm a bloody joke. Look at me."

He avoids looking at me, looking in every direction but directly at me, obviously because I'm so fucking hideous now.

I continue my rant, "Look at my arms, for starters. They're at least two feet shorter. My knuckles used to drag quite comfortably along the ground when I stood up straight. Now my arms don't even reach past my knees. I'm gonna have to bend over to pick stuff up off the floor. What a bloody chore."

How do humans not break, having to bend over so far every time they drop something?

My hands explore my face once more. I don't need to see the result to know it feels all wrong.

"My teeth are all straight. And my lovely monobrow, it's split in two. My nose 'as shrunk an' all." I screech, almost hysterical as I discover more and more changes. "And where's all my bloody hair gone? How do humans not freeze to bloody death?"

"You have hair." Lucien regards me with a frown. "On your head, your chest, your arms, your legs and erm, your erm…" He waves his hands in the direction of my groin.

I look down in confusion and suddenly realise why he seems to be finding it difficult to look at me. It's not because I'm hideous; it's because I'm bloody naked.

Well of course I am. I'm a troll, but usually everything is covered in a thick layer of black fur. Now all that's covering me is a sprinkling of curly black hairs here and there, while the rest of my dark skin is available for public viewing. It's a bloody good job the bridge is deserted this time of night.

"Bloody hell," I exclaim, covering my essentials with my hands and giving an involuntary shiver. I give Lucien a helpless look.

He seems to be having some sort of battle with his emotions. Is he trying not to laugh? The prissy little bastard.

"Here, let me help you," he says with a light snort.

He gives a seemingly nonchalant wave of his hand. There's a soft noise, like a gentle wind through leaves. I look down at myself and suddenly I'm clothed. I never felt a thing.

"Bloody hell, Fairy Boy. That was smooth." I grunt in appreciation. Credit where credit's due, although I don't know why he would wait until now to do it when it was that easy.

Lucien flicks his eyebrows, clicks his tongue and winks at me. I don't know what sort of effect he was hoping that would have on me as a troll, but it seems to have caused some sort of physical reaction in me as a human. Trolls don't blush, but my cheeks have just heated to roasting. Hopefully, my dark skin hides the fact, because I'm at a loss to explain why his winking at me has made me blush.

I examine the clothes Lucien's conjured up for me, mostly in order to avoid looking him in the eye, but also out of curiosity. I don't know what humans wear nowadays. The last time I spent any decent amount of time above ground, humans were wearing some sort of animal skin, tied at the waist with rope. What I'm wearing now is a far cry from that. The clothes are comfortable: a soft, loose-fitting top and warm, slightly baggy trousers. I suppose I should be grateful for that. He could have given me something made of raw wool that would itch like hell for the next forty-eight hours.

I shiver. The enormity of the task fills me with sudden dread. There must have been thousands of locks hanging on my bridge. Humans have been leaving them there for decades. I glance around me. The locks have all disappeared.

"Where'd they all go?" I exclaim in utter surprise. "The locks I mean."

"They have been taken for processing, Monsieur Troll," Lucien explains.

"What the 'ell does that mean? And 'ow am I supposed to fix them all if they ain't here?" I groan. I'm going to be stuck in this human body forever. I shiver again, wrapping my significantly shorter arms around my torso. I miss my fur.

"Monsieur, you are cold?" Lucien lays a gentle hand on my arm. I frown down at it. He's being very attentive. Why?

"B-bloody f-freezing," I try to say through chattering teeth.

Despite the clothes he has conjured up for me, I'm just not used to feeling the cool air on my skin. My fur may have been thick, black, matted and dirty, but it protected me from the cold. It also belonged to me. I feel like it's all been stolen, which it has. I'm more than a little angry about that.

"We should go somewhere warmer." Lucien looks around him, giving a small shiver himself. "Come, we still have a few hours before full dawn. My apartment is not far from here. We can rest there, get a warm drink and perhaps something to eat. I will explain everything to you."

My anger is replaced by indecision. I need his help, even if I don't want it. I don't want to be stuck like this for the rest of eternity, and I don't have a fucking clue where to start with fixing the locks. I have to find the buggers first. I still don't understand why what I did was so bad. Anyway, I need Lucien, but he's also suggesting I leave my bridge. I haven't done that in a very long time.

"Not far you say?" I continue to scowl, if only to hide the mild panic I'm feeling at venturing any further than the end of my bridge.

"It is alongside the river," Lucien assures me, pointing. "On the other side of Ile de la Cité." He smiles in what I think is an attempt at reassurance—a good one, because as he gently takes my hand, I suddenly feel as if I would be safe following him anywhere.

Chapter 3: Locked in the City

A s we walk, I can't help gaping at the buildings around us. The last time I ventured away from my bridge, this place was little more than a collection of wooden huts and dirt tracks. I knew things had changed, but despite living here almost my entire, long, troll life, I am a stranger in a strange land. It's a culture shock.

It's all a bit—I don't know—grey. Everywhere is built up. At least when there were just muddy paths and huts, there was a bit of space. Now everything feels closed in. Not that I mind being closed in. I'm a seven foot troll who lives in a hole underneath a dirty old bridge. Cramped living space is my norm, but this—this is different. The place looks uncared for. There's litter everywhere, and someone's gone and drawn over everything. Talk about lack of respect. If they did that to my bridge I'd bloody eat 'em.

Thankfully, there aren't that many people about this time of night/early morning. So they can't see me gaping at everything, like an uncultured country bumpkin. Lucien sees, though, and I can see he is finding it rather amusing, the annoying sod that he is.

"All righ', Fairy Boy, you can stop laughing at the uneducated buffoon. We can't all be sophisticated city slickers."

Lucien snorts, and my lips twitch with the urge to laugh along with him.

"I am not sophisticated, Monsieur Troll, and I do not think you are uneducated, or a buffoon." His expression is bright, as always. Nothing seems to faze him. He gets angry, but it never lasts long. He stops and regards me with his head tipped to one side, his lips pursed as his eyes study my face. "Look, I cannot keep calling you Monsieur Troll. What is your name?"

"My what?"

"Your name? When you were born, you weren't named Troll. If every troll was named Troll, that would be terribly confusing. What is your given name? I have not been able to find any mention of it in l'Authoritié archives."

I stare at him as if he has two heads. For all I know, I could have the double cranium. I still haven't seen a reflection of the monstrosity I've become. He asked my name, though. I'm a bit taken aback.

"You probably can't find any mention of it because no one ever asked me my name before."

"What? No one?" Fairy boy looks shocked—horrified, in fact.

"No. No one was ever interested."

"I'm interested." His expression is clear and earnest. His blue eyes sparkle.

What the heck. I might as well tell him my name, even if our acquaintance is only going to last for forty-eight hours.

"Alright then, it's Sol." I shrug.

"Sol the Troll?" Lucien snorts, then gasps and bites his lip to stop himself from laughing. "Oh, that was terribly rude of me, I'm sorry. I didn't mean to laugh."

"Yeah, well, at least my name rhymes. Not like yours, Lucien the Fairy. What's the point of having a name that doesn't rhyme?"

"Names do not have to rhyme, Sol. Who on Earth told you that?"

"Er, that'd be my mum, Lol."

"Ha, lol, I knew you were joking." He punches my shoulder, and I wobble a little, since he packs a punch despite his size. He's giggling. His laugh is a bit infectious, but I'm not sure what he's laughing at. Why does he think I'm joking?

"What's so funny about my mum?" I ask, and he immediately stops laughing with another gasp.

"Oh, again, I am terribly sorry. I thought you meant…not… Your maman is called…" He isn't smiling now, he looks mortified. Unhappy that he could have insulted me. I like it better when he's smiling. How can I make that happen again?

We continue to walk while I think. He leads me, his hand, amazingly, still holding mine, as if he's afraid I'll float away or something equally ridiculous. It anchors me in this unfamiliar city. I don't want to admit I'm well out of my comfort zone even this short distance from my bridge, but I am well out of my comfort zone.

"Do all Troll names rhyme with troll?" Lucien asks after a short period of silence. His question is hesitant, as if he's afraid I'll bite his head off. I've never actually done that. I have been known to get snappy with unwanted visitors, but I never actually ate any of them.

I really wasn't that offended by Lucien's laughter. Answering his questions will distract me from the panic attack that is lurking just beneath my gruff, bad-tempered exterior.

"'Course they do. Don't you know anything?"

"You really are having a joke with me, now, surely?" Lucien narrows his eyes in suspicion. It makes me laugh.

"No I ain't. There's Nol, and Gol, and Fol that used to live down river on the toll bridge." I list them on my fingers. "They're all gone now. Then there was my aunty Jol and uncle Zol. My dad's name was Mol." It's beginning to sound a little silly now, even I'll admit, and I can see Lucien is beginning to lose his grip. Tears of laughter sparkle in his eyes, but he's doing a good job of keeping a straight face. "Come to think of it, our names are pretty ridiculous. It's a good job there's not that many of us or we'd run out of alphabet and things really would get confusing."

"I still think you're telling me porkies." Lucien snorts.

"No I ain't, straight up. All our names rhyme with troll."

"Heaven forbid if my name had to rhyme. I'd end up with something ludicrous like Hairy Fairy."

I snort. "Hairy Fairy." I reach out and flick his shock of auburn curls. "It'd suit ya, since you've got more hair than me now. I'm gonna call you that from now on, just because you laughed at my name."

Lucien huffs and turns away but not before I see a smile touch the corner of his pink lips. There, I did it. I made him smile again. I'm definitely using that nickname.

Goodness' sake what's the matter with me? Since when did it matter in the slightest whether Fairy Boy here smiles or not? I couldn't give a bloody monkey's fart. I just want to go back to hiding in my troll home. But I can't do that until I'm a troll again.

"Monsieur Troll." Lucien touches my arm, and I almost jump a mile.

His touch is like a bolt of lightning. Bloody hell. It must be the fact there's no bloody fur on my arm, or at least not enough to cover any decent troll.

"Je suis desole. Mais, nous sommes ici, mon cheri." He grimaces and gives an embarrassed chuckle as he bites his lip. "Er, I mean we are here, Sol. My home."

I stare down at him blankly for a few seconds, because it's a bit of an assault on my senses, all of this, and I'm not just talking about walking through the city streets. That's bad enough. It's everything else as well. His touch sets my skin on fire. I had no idea human skin was so sensitive. Hearing my name said out loud, for the first time in who knows how long, is just another thing my fuddled brain has to process.

It takes me a while to register that we have stopped and that he is trying to pull me into an open doorway.

"You live here?" I am a bit surprised, because I thought fairies lived in trees, and you entered their homes through little secret doorways hidden in the roots. Shows how much I know. "But this looks like a human home."

"It is." Lucien pulls me into a spacious entrance hall. "Humans live here too. There are six apartments in this building."

"Do your neighbours know you're a fairy, then?" I am curious to know how that works.

"Do your neighbours know you are a troll?" His comeback is quick and throws me off balance as he leads me up some stairs.

"I don't have any neighbours, Hairy. Unless you wanna count the ducks."

Lucien looks very sad for some reason. "Don't you ever get lonely?" he asks me, without meeting my eye.

"No!" I scowl. I don't need his pity, and that sounded very much like pity. "I don't have time to get lonely. I spend most of it sleeping." He regards me with surprise. "Trolls sleep a lot."

I avoid his gaze until he pulls me inside his apartment and then I go back to staring about me in wonder. This is very different from my troll house. It's much cleaner, for starters.

"I live in a human home because we are encouraged to fit in as much as possible with the humans we protect," Lucien explains.

I frown. "Protect? From what?"

"From dark magic, spells that go wrong, mischief makers." I don't miss the significant look he gives me after that last item on his list. "Monsters, creatures and things that go bump in the night," he adds with a grin.

"You mean like me?" I regard him with a nod.

"You are not a monster, Sol." He searches my face in concern. "I do not think so anyway."

"Meaning others do."

"They just do not know you."

"You don't know me either." I raise my eyebrows. He continues to grin but is a little less sure of himself.

Maybe he's beginning to regret inviting a troll into his nice home. Not that I'm planning on doing anything bad—just trolls and nice things don't mix, and Lucien's home is definitely a nice thing.

I look around his living room with appreciation. It's all very neat and tidy, something I could never aspire to. Perhaps, when this is all over, he'll help me get my home tidied up a bit. I've never been that good at housework.

What am I saying? When this is all over he's not going to want anything to do with me. I'll go back to my hole and hibernate, and he and all his fairy bureaucrat friends will go back to keeping an eye on me from a safe distance.

Lucien pulls me further into his home and towards a wide window that is the entire width and height of one wall of his living room. Panic begins to tighten a knot in my stomach. Everything that's been going on has been enough distraction to get me up here without thinking, but now it's been pointed out to me, all I can think about is how many stairs we've just climbed. I feel a bit sick.

Lucien's panoramic window looks out over the river, which would be a source of comfort to me if we weren't so bloody high up. I take some deep breaths and try not to look, but Lucien seems intent on showing me the view, oblivious to my growing panic.

"See, I told you we would not be far from the river. You have a good view of it here."

"Er—yeah, it's great, Lucien. Fantastic." I am pointedly not looking at the window.

"How can you even see it, Sol? You have your eyes closed." I can hear his voice is close, but I can't open my eyes, because if I do I think I'll vomit, or pass out. Trolls are not supposed to be any higher than ground level. Lower than that is preferable.

"Oh dear." I can feel my legs giving way beneath me.

"Sol!" Lucien exclaims before I feel his hands on my arms. He urges me backwards, and when I feel the backs of my legs hit the soft cushions of his sofa, I sit heavily, still not opening my eyes. "Sol, what is wrong? Are you ill? Open your eyes, speak to me, s'il vous plait, mon cheri."

"I'm fine, Lucien," I lie. I mustn't sound too convincing, because he clicks his tongue and lays a cool, soft hand on my forehead.

"You are very pale, but you do not have a fever. You do feel a little cold. Here." He pulls a warm blanket around me. "I will make you a warm drink. That is why we came here, n'est pas?"

"Yeah." I can feel my breathing getting back to normal. I'm sitting down now, so I won't be able to see how high we are. I take a chance and open my eyes.

I'm facing the window, but thankfully, all I can see is sky. Sky is good. Anything higher than me is good. The blanket is soft and warm, and Lucien's fingers are massaging my temples. That is also good.

I moan.

What the hell?

"Is it the transformation? Is it still affecting you? Or do you need to eat? Is that why you are dizzy?" I groan again as Lucien continues to list possible reasons for my dizzy spell. He's growing more and more concerned by the second. "Sol, parle moi, mon cheri. Est ce—"

I stop him with a hand on his arm. He's near hysterical and jabbering in French. I'm going to have to admit the real reason. He's going to think I'm a right wimp, but I can't let him carry on like this.

"Hairy, it ain't any of the things you've just said. It's the bloody height of your bloody apartment."

"La taille?" He frowns, and I watch him out of the corner of my eye as he stands to look out of his panoramic window. "We are only on the third floor, Sol."

"Bloody 'ell." Even the thought of him looking out of the window is making me feel sick, and I fight the urge to pull him back. As if he's going to fall, and as if he'd be in any danger even if he did. He's a bloody fairy. "It's all right fer you. You're a fairy." I close my eyes again and hope the wave of nausea will pass. "You've got wings an' all that crap. Being up high isn't a problem when you've got wings. Me, I'm a troll. I prefer to 'ave my feet firmly on the ground, at ground level, or lower if possible."

"Monsieur Troll." I feel the sofa dip slightly as Lucien sits back down beside me. "Sol." He lays a gentle hand on my arm, and I can feel all the dizziness and panic evaporating. He must be using some sort of subtle spell that I can't hear, because only magic would have me feeling better so fast. "I am sorry, mon cheri, I did not think when I brought you up here. You did not seem bothered by the stairs."

I wasn't bothered by the stairs, because I had other things distracting me, like how my human body was reacting to his touch and his smile and his breath on my cheek. His breath is on my cheek now, then he's bloody kissing my cheek and the sensations are just too much to process. I think I'm going to pass out. That spell he's using is powerful stuff, I feel all warm and safe. And now he's massaging my shoulders. It all feels too nice.

"Lucien, gawd, I'm fine. Gerroff me, will ya?" I brush his hands away. "Go and make that drink and let me just sit. Sitting's good."

"Bien." He smiles at me, and the floating sensation continues. "I will make hot chocolate, I think."

I nod in agreement, because right now he could suggest I drink my own urine and I wouldn't give a shit. I'm high on the spell he's just woven to make me feel better.

"Hot chocolate?" I ask as he walks away to his open plan kitchen. "What the 'ell's that?"

"It is a drink, Sol. Have you never had hot chocolate?" He sounds surprised.

"No, I drink river water."

"Oh!" Now he sounds a little disgusted. Well, sod him. Fairies, they're all bloody snobs, even when they try to act like they're not.

"I never needed any fancy stuff, Hairy."

"I can get you some river water, if you like." He offers, and he doesn't even sound like he's kidding.

I twist so I'm at a better angle to see him. By his earnest expression, it looks like his offer is genuine, like he'd actually go all the way down to the river to get me some water to drink. I don't understand why he'd go to such lengths to make me feel at home.

I don't want him to make such an effort. We seem to have some sort of tentative acquaintance going on here, and it's a new experience for me after being alone for most of my life. I don't want him to think I'm some sort of diva. I need his help, and besides, I would quite like to taste this hot chocolate he's making.

"It's all right, Hairy. I'll try some of yer chocolate stuff, thanks."

"Trés bien!" He smiles brightly and turns back to his bench, where he fusses over mugs and pans and what looks like milk. Oh, I like milk. I've only had it a few times, and since the incident with the goats I haven't touched the stuff, but if hot chocolate is made with milk, it can't be that bad can it?

"What was that spell you used on me?" I call to him without moving my head. I still feel quite warm and relaxed. "It was pretty potent."

"I did not cast any spell, Sol," he calls back, sounding a little confused.

Well that's weird.

A few minutes later, Lucien hands me a steaming mug and sits right beside me on the sofa. This closeness he seems to favour, it can only be because I'm in this human form, surely. If I was in my troll form, I doubt he'd even allow me in his home. It's cosy, though. I suppose I can allow myself to enjoy it while it lasts.

"So tell me what we 'ave to do to fix these locks then. We may as well get started on the explanations while we drink." I take a sip of the chocolate and gasp. "Blimey, that's really nice."

"Of course it's nice," Lucien preens. "I made it." He gives me an artless grin, and I chuckle. "Now, about the locks." He gets down to business. "As I said, they have been taken for processing. Not every lock is still active. They are being sorted right now. Once they are, it will be easier to explain to you on the job, so to speak. You are already assigned a quota of locks to fix, and the rest will be assigned to other teams."

"Teams?" I give him a bemused look. "How many others are doing this?"

"There are many helping to restore the locks, Sol. Time is of the essence. Everyone has been pulled from their assignments and all leave has been cancelled."

"Oh! Bloody hell. I bet I'm popular right now."

Lucien chuckles. "Sol, did you think you would have to do it all by yourself?" He gives me a slightly sympathetic look when I nod. "It would take one person ten lifetimes to restore all of those locks by themselves. It will be difficult enough to fix one hundred. That is why we must all work in pairs."

"And who's the lucky bastard that gets stuck with me then?" I wonder if we're just waiting for that unfortunate sod to turn up and hold my hand throughout the entire process.

"Er, that would be me." Lucien frowns, as if he cannot understand my sarcastic tone.

"Blimey." I grimace. "That must've been one helluva short straw you drew there, Hairy." I laugh at the unfairness that has him stuck with me when there are hundreds of other, far more capable partners he could have had. "Who did you piss off to get that job?"

"I did not piss off anyone, Sol." He frowns as he continues to sip at his chocolate. It must be a little too hot because his cheeks are flushed. "I asked to be your partner."

Without meeting my eye and without another word, he gets up and takes his and my empty mugs back to his kitchen, while I stare at him in complete bewilderment.

"You asked?" I splutter. I turn so I can see him clattering around in his kitchen. "Why the 'ell would you do that?"

"Because I did." He does not elaborate. He looks uncomfortable, actually. I might go as far as to say he looks embarrassed.

I can't think about that right now, because that hot drink has gone straight through me, and I need to go, really badly. I'm going to have to risk catching a glimpse of the far-too-high view in order to find Lucien's bathroom. I'm pretty certain he won't be happy with me pissing out of the window, like I do at home. Besides I doubt I'd hit the river from here, and I'd run the risk of vomiting as well if I got too close to that view.

With slightly wobbly legs, I get to my feet, keeping my eyes on Lucien and not on the window looming behind me.

"Where's your bathroom, Hairy?" I ask, walking around the sofa.

"Oh, here, I will help you." Lucien rushes to my side, but I brush him off.

"Oy, I can manage the bathroom on my own, thanks. Just tell me where it is."

"Fine." He huffs, pointing at a door. "Through there and first right."

I think he watches me leave, but I don't turn around. What is it with him? He actually volunteered to partner me on this thing, even though I must have caused him enough trouble already and then he gets cross when I refuse his help.

Fairies, I'll never understand them. I mean, who would ask to work with me? I'm an ugly, hairy black troll—oh!

What the hell? There's someone else in here with me.

"Bloody fairy bollocks. Who the bloody hell are you?" I shout out before I realise what I'm actually looking at. It's a mirror.

It's not often I find myself in a bathroom. I can't remember the last time I saw my own reflection, apart from a distorted image in the surface of the river.

I peer at the image in the mirror, and he peers back. Is that what I look like as a human? Bloody hell. I'm all—smooth—and my skin is as dark as the chocolate I've just had to drink.

The shirt I'm wearing is pulled slightly taut over a chest that I never realised was so muscular. The hair on the top of my head isn't fur, it's like proper human hair—tight, black curls and still messy, but good messy.

I turn my head from side to side. Lucien is right. I do have hair, just not as much as before. I've got just enough to say I'm hairy, but ruggedly hairy.

"Sol, are you all right? I heard you call out." Lucien's voice through the door startles me, and I quickly look away. I've got more important things to do than admire myself in front of a mirror.

"I'm fine, Hairy." I snort softly at the irony of the nickname, since it turns out I'm still hairier than him. I bet he doesn't have any hairs on his chest. I've got tons. "I'll be out soon."

"Non, non, mon cheri. Take as long as you need. I have had a message from L'Authoritié de Fée Folklorique. The locks have been processed, and the teams are being sent out immediately. We can start fixing them whenever you are ready."

Well, that news puts a spark in my step. I finish what I have to do and rush out into Lucien's living room. I'm in such a rush, I forget how small his apartment is. I collide with him, and because I'm still not used to the way my human limbs move, we land in an ungraceful heap on his floor. I'm on top, with him struggling beneath me—again.

This time, I have a little more insight into what I'm feeling when his vibrant, lithe body wriggles against mine. My breath catches in my throat, and he stops struggling with a soft gasp.

I look down at him. His eyes are wide, and his chest is heaving. Is he afraid? I don't want him to be. For the first time in my life, I don't want to be the scary, horrible, grumpy old troll.

"We 'ave to stop meetin' like this, Hairy." I try to inject some humour into what is becoming a serious situation—for me, anyway.

He gives a soft huff, and his eyes twinkle with amusement, the fear gone from them. They're very pretty eyes. His hair frames his head, spread out around him like a circle of flame. Lucien is quite simply the most beautiful creature I've ever seen. But he won't ever be mine. Not in a million years.

I'm getting all sorts of signals from places in my body I never got signals from before, and they're all very nice signals. But it has to stop.

With a mumbled apology, and flaming hot cheeks I push myself away.

Lucien quickly and nimbly jumps to his feet, brushing himself down and straightening his clothes. I'm a little slower, and there's another problem I need to deal with—something I'd rather wasn't quite so straight.

Clearing my throat I turn away from him. He didn't seem to be as affected as me, just a little shocked. He doesn't need to know I can't keep this body's libido under control every time he so much as touches me.

"Alright, Hairy, tell me where we 'ave to go to fix these locks. Have they got them stored somewhere?" I need a major distraction, and being so close to achieving my goal is proving enough.

I turn back to face him, and he straightens quickly, biting his lip. His face is as pink as the ice cream he was eating when we first met. Maybe he is more affected than I thought. He reaches out to me and whispers my name, a look of wonder in his eyes.

I'm not really any good at this sort of thing. I've lived in relative isolation for over two thousand years. I want to apologise to him, but my default setting, as a troll, is grumpiness.

"Are we gonna get on with this lock thing or not, Hairy?" I snap at him irritably. "Because it seems to me like we've wasted enough time with all this fluff." I wave my hands about his apartment, and he scowls.

"Of course." He snatches up a messenger bag and throws it over his head so the strap sits across his chest, then walks to the door and opens it. He taps his foot impatiently. "Come on then, Monsieur Troll, let's not waste any more time."

Chapter 4: Locked in a Café

W HY ARE WE here, Hairy?" I ask through gritted teeth, my body sizzling with frustration.

We are sitting in a pavement café having breakfast of all things. Lucien said we were going to fix love locks, but I haven't seen any locks, or any indication that there's any around to fix.

So far, all I've managed to achieve is almost getting us kicked out of the café when I loomed over the waiter and asked him what his problem was. I didn't know he was waiting to take our order. I've never been in a café before.

So we're just sitting now, with cups of what Lucien says is coffee, and tastes kind of bitter and makes my head buzz, and something he called a croissant, which is a bit tasty, actually. I could eat ten. We haven't seen anyone with any locks though. What the hell is going on?

"We are waiting, Sol. You must be patient." Lucien is looking about him, his keen, sharp eyes taking in everything and everyone around us. He's fascinating to watch, but much as I am enjoying watching him, we have a job to do, and time is running away with us.

Not only that, but I feel like a fish out of water. Trolls aren't supposed to sit in stylish cafés, eating croissants and drinking coffee. I know I currently don't look anything like a troll, but that fact doesn't dispel any of the self-consciousness. I am absolutely convinced that everyone is staring at us. I look around with a scowl, and people quickly find their coffee cups very interesting. Everyone *was* staring at us. Bloody hell.

I suppose we do make a bit of an odd couple. He's so tiny and fluffy, and I'm so tall and bloody prickly as hell. I'm just waiting for someone to walk over and tell me I don't belong.

"What is it exactly that you're looking for?" I follow his gaze as it settles on a human couple sitting in the opposite corner of the café. As we watch, they reach across the table and take each other's hands, gazing lovingly into each other's eyes. Lucien looks away with a frustrated huff.

"They are here. I can sense it." He slaps the table irritably and then meets my gaze as I watch him in bemusement. "What?" He scowls so I scowl back.

"What do you mean, what? You said the locks were ready for fixing, yet here we are, eating breakfast and people watching, like we have all the time in the world. And you still haven't explained how we're going to fix them—just that it isn't as simple as pushing them shut again. I don't know what the hell that's supposed to mean, Hairy."

"Oh, will you please stop calling me that?" he hisses irritably, and totally out of character, or at least the character I was beginning to get to know.

"I-I'm sorry, Hai—er, I mean, Lucien." I feel on edge, nervous and out of place and I just want to get on with the job so things can go back to the way they were. I'm not good up here. Trolls live under bridges. They don't socialise. This one doesn't, anyway.

To make things worse, Lucien has been snippy with me since we left his apartment. He seems on edge as well, and his mood is making me feel more and more nervous. I can't make too much of a fuss about it all, since I need his help to do this task, otherwise I'll be stuck as a human and quite possibly homeless. I clasp my hands together on the table in front of me and try to force myself to relax.

Lucien hangs his head with a sigh and covers my hands with his. The shock that shoots up my arms at his touch causes me to gasp and swallow hard. Is this what it's like for humans every time they make physical contact? Come to think of it, I've not had that much experience with physical contact as a troll, so maybe it's like this for me in any form. Bloody hell. It's better to stay isolated and alone than to feel this mishmash of emotions every time someone so much as brushes their fingers across my skin.

"I'm sorry, Sol. I should not have snapped." Lucien searches my face with an apologetic smile and then he looks away, biting his bottom lip. "And I don't really mind you calling me Hairy." He sighs again and goes back to watching the few occupants of the café. "It's the unfairness of all of this that has me so uptight."

Ah. Now we're getting to the truth of it. He says he volunteered to be partnered with me, but did he really, or was he pushed?

"The way you have been treated over this has been dreadful. You have lived here for over two thousand years and no one in l'AFF even bothered to record your name. I couldn't find any record of it."

So that's what he means by unfair. He's angry about that, rather than his own situation. I'm a little taken aback that he would feel so passionately about it.

"I told ya, Hairy. No one ever came and asked me. Although when I first started living underneath that bridge, there wasn't any authority of fairies, or anything like that. There was no one to ask if it was okay to live there, and the human residents ran a mile every time I tried. They made up stories about me to frighten their kids, so I decided it was best to just stay out of their way. Your fairy bureaucrats all arrived during one of my long hibernations, and after I tried speaking to them a few times and got no joy, I decided grumpy and sullen was the best way to act in order to be left alone."

"I am sorry for their failings, Sol. Les fées should have tried harder. When I began to watch your bridge, the only thing I was told was to steer clear of you, as if you were dangerous and weren't to be disturbed. I knew that could not be true, you had lived there for so long and never caused any problems. The more

I watched you, the more I realised you weren't trouble, just lonely, and it made me want to reach out, not steer clear."

I try to ignore the lump in my throat. I should default to my grumpy state and snap at him, but somehow his concern for me has touched a part of me I thought had died a long time ago—a part that has never really been touched by anyone before. He kept watch over my bridge because he doubted the stories. This one's different, for sure.

"Thanks," I say quietly. "You're the only one that seems to think that."

"I am trying to change minds, but there are such stories about you. I spoke to my—I mean Madame Queen, after she had changed you. I tried to plead your side of the story, but she would not listen. She said it was time you earned your keep."

I look up in shock. "What's that supposed to mean? Bloody hell, Hairy. That bridge is mine. It was mine long before your lot came along and started to regulate everything. I wasn't bothering no one. All I want is to live in peace. I couldn't even do that, because your lot had allowed some sort of human ritual of locking their love up in a padlock all over the bloody place. I tried to tell someone about it, but no one listened."

"I know." Lucien frowns. "I looked in the archives, and there is no record of you ever speaking to anyone in l'AFF."

I stand and lean over the table, my face close to his. "Then your lot are 'avin' a laff, because I spoke to loads of bloody fairies, all with bloody clipboards. They all nodded, then backed away and never came back. I gave up in the end and went into hibernation, except I couldn't properly because of the noise of them bloody padlocks."

"Sol!" Lucien grabs my arm, and at first I think it's to stop me storming out, because I was about to do just that, but then I see his expression is one of barely contained excitement. "Sol, look. They are here."

I frown as I sit back down. Following his gaze, I see a couple. They look like any other couple sitting in this café, except…there is just something different, something I can't put my finger on.

"Who are they, Lucien?" Are they the ones with the locks? Is my task about to start properly?

"They are the ones we came here for. Look at them. They are broken, Sol, can you not see?"

I can see. That's what's different. I see the break, as if it's physical. They don't meet each other's eyes. They don't touch, as others are touching. They don't even speak to each other, and they look unhappy as hell.

"What's wrong with them?" I whisper, not wanting to disturb the fragile atmosphere that seems to have formed around us and the couple.

"Yesterday, they were the happiest they could ever have been, but this morning they woke up and something had changed. They could not remember the reason they were together. Something was broken, but because they are human they do not understand what. They cannot hope to comprehend the complexities of the magic of love."

"You what?" I have no idea what he's talking about. I just gape at him.

"Sol." He sighs, turning back to me and taking my hands in his again. The sensation isn't quite so shocking, but it still makes my skin tingle. "This is why we are here. You thought we would be handed a box full of open padlocks, and all we would have to do was close them again, yes?"

I nod. He shakes his head.

"Non, mon cheri. We have to seal the love back inside those locks, and to do that we have to find the couple that each lock belongs to."

"Then what?" I still don't get it.

"Then we must fix what is broken."

41

"What I broke, you mean." I think I'm beginning to understand the magnitude of this undertaking and the damage my selfish act has caused. "How are we supposed to fix it, then?"

I look back over at the couple. Happy as Larry, they were yesterday, Lucien says. It doesn't look like it today. They look desperately miserable, as if they are simply going through the motions of being together. I have no idea how I know that, because I know nothing about relationships, but I can sense it. Maybe it's being in close proximity to a fairy. They know all about that fluffy, pink, feathery stuff.

"We must find their moment, Sol," Lucien explains, still watching the couple intently.

"Their what?"

"Their moment. The moment when they fell in love." He has a wistful, faraway look in his eyes. I can't help the laugh that explodes from my mouth. This is just so stupid.

"Bwahahahaha! Hairy. Tell me another one."

Lucien's scowl makes me laugh even harder.

"I am not telling jokes, Sol. This is serious. Your home is at stake here—and your status as a troll, if you are stuck in this form. I am trying to help you. The least you can do is not laugh in my face." He folds his arms over his chest and narrows his eyes angrily.

I swallow the next chuckle and nod. This is for my sake. I should listen to him.

"I'm sorry. I know you're trying to help me. I don't know why you would want to, but at least you're still here." I heave a sigh. I really don't know how I haven't been left high and dry already. He's one determined little fairy, this one, and I am very grateful, even if I'm not very good at showing it. "So you were saying, about finding their moment? How do we do that? Is it difficult?"

"Sometimes it is, and sometimes it isn't." He shrugs. "Love does not always happen for everyone at the same time. We need to find the moment they both realised they were in love with each other."

"And how do we do that?" I'm feeling a little weak just thinking about how difficult this is going to be. "Do we go and speak to them? Ask them outright?"

Lucien shakes his head. "Non, cheri, we must search their memories. Awaken the one that has been forgotten. When they remember together, the lock will be resealed."

"You mean we don't even have to touch the lock?"

Lucien shakes his head. I sit back in my seat, blowing out my cheeks. How am I supposed to help Lucien with this?

"Lucien, I can't search people's memories. I don't know how."

"It is not difficult. Don't worry, mon cheri. I will show you how."

He holds out his hand, and I regard it for a moment. The sensations that shoot through my body every time he touches me aren't unpleasant, but they are very distracting if I'm supposed to be concentrating on something else. I take his hand, and he smiles.

"Now close your eyes."

Oh hell! Closing my eyes is only going to intensify the sensory overload.

~*Can you hear me, mon cheri?*

"Bloody hell!" I open my eyes again, because if his physical touch is too much for me, his mental touch threatens to send me sky high. I grab the table to keep me from flying off into the rafters.

"Close your eyes and concentrate, Sol." Lucien clicks his tongue. He doesn't seem to notice that he almost needed to peel me from the ceiling.

I do as I'm told.

~*Now, can you hear me?*

~*Yes.*

~*Concentrate, Sol.*

~I'll try.

This is strange. I feel detached, like I'm not a part of my body anymore. Everything is a little out of focus and fuzzy around the edges. Noises are muffled. When I look around, I can see the table we were sitting at. Lucien is there, holding hands with some, tall, dark-skinned bloke with messy hair. I experience an irrational flash of jealousy until I realise it's me. I'm looking at myself.

I pull from Lucien's hand in panic. Something pulls me backwards, like it's attached at my navel. I open my eyes to find I am sitting back at the table, and Lucien is regarding me with just a hint of frustration in his eyes.

I grimace in apology. I'm a bit embarrassed that I panicked so easily. It's not as if I don't know what telepathy and astral projection are. I'm a magical creature, for heaven's sake. I was born knowing these things. I'm angry with myself for reacting like an amateur, but also a bit confused. What the hell was I jealous of?

"Focus!" Lucien tells me, and then holds out his hands to me again.

He doesn't seem as flustered, like he's done this a thousand times. He may be frustrated with my inexperience, but he also has this air of patience and warmth about him. As my gaze is caught by his clear blue eyes, I suddenly trust him beyond measure. I close my eyes and follow his thoughts, a silvery thread, guiding me towards the broken lovers we are trying to 'fix'.

~We must stay in physical contact. It will keep our minds linked together. We need to separate our thoughts and search the memories of each individual, until we find one they both share.

~How will I know I've found the right one?

~You will know.

He's being a bit cryptic, but words are not the only way to share information in this form of communication. I sense his emotions too, and the unspoken words, as if reading between the lines—if I'd ever bothered to learn to read.

~You don't know how to read?

~Now who's the one that needs to focus?

~Stop thinking so much, Sol, and maybe I'll be able to.

I focus on the mind I am invading. I know that's not strictly true. I'm not in there to take over, and they'll never know I was there, but it still feels like an invasion of their privacy. I don't even know what it is I'm looking for, so I'm going to have to search through everything.

It's a female mind. Ordered but chaotic at the same time, full of lists of things to do that never get done because there's always something more important.

~Blimey, it's like getting lost inside a maze.

~Concentrate on the emotions, Sol. Look for positive ones, avoid the negative.

~What happens if I find a negative one?

~You could get caught up in it, and sometimes it isn't pretty.

~Blimey!

I'd better concentrate then.

There's a lot of colour, encasing memories like shiny bubbles. It's like a rainbow in here, except, there's this one little bubble, hiding in the background that isn't full of colour. It's grey.

~I didn't know you could get grey bubbles.

~That's it, Sol. The grey one. Don't let it out of your sight.

I do as he says. It's not difficult. It kind of stands out, even though it's smaller and looks a little shrivelled. It's all deflated and...

~Look inside for me, Sol. See if it is the same memory as I have found.

I get closer and peer inside. It's like looking through frosted glass, or trying to look through ice to see the river below.

Inside, it's not what I expected at all. The way Lucien was talking, this 'moment' seemed monumental, but what I see is a really normal, domestic activity. The couple are sorting their washing. One holds a basket while the other hangs the wet clothes out on the line.

When I spent more time above ground, back in centuries gone by, it was an activity I saw quite a lot.

~*How can someone fall in love over a washing line? I mean, that's not very romantic.*

~*Hush, Sol. We have found their moment. Let them see it, bring it forward.*

I do as he asks, and suddenly the bubble inflates and is enveloped in a myriad of colours. In the same instant, I hear a resounding click in my ears. It's so loud, I lose my concentration and am pulled back into my body with a jerk.

"Bugger me!" I'm pulled with such force my chair tips precariously before thudding back into position.

My exclamation attracts attention, and a woman regards me with disapproval.

"What you lookin' at?" I growl at her, forgetting I'm not a troll.

She looks away with a gasp.

"Sol!" Lucien reprimands.

"Sorry!" I huff. I give the woman one more scowl before turning my attention back to Lucien. Now *I* gasp. He's regarding me with slight amusement, but he's also glowing with excitement.

"So, that was your first lock. What did you think?" He is practically jumping out of his seat. And now people are staring at *him*.

"Are they all that easy?" I raise my eyebrows and act nonchalant, polishing my fingernails on the collar of my shirt.

Lucien narrows his eyes. "Were you not excited to hear that click? It is one click closer to regaining your true form."

"Alright, I was, a bit," I admit. "Although it might've been nice to actually know what the hell was going on."

"I told you it was easier to show you. It would have taken me too long to explain it."

"Meaning you didn't think I'd understand." I fold my arms across my chest. "I might be an illiterate troll, but I understand more than you think, Fairy Boy."

That woman is watching us again. The same one as before. I sneer at her, and she turns away with another gasp. I look around and everyone is staring at us again.

"Oy, this ain't a circus. We'll start chargin' a fee next." Everyone turns away. It's like we're the main attraction.

"Sol." Lucien chuckles. His excitement is still affecting him, and I watch as his eyes twinkle with mirth. "Such a charmer. Let's go before we get kicked out."

With a giggle, he stands, takes my hand and pulls me to my feet.

I'm caught up in his excitement too. I ignore his jibe at my lack of charm and join in with his giggling as he pulls me out of the café.

As we leave, I glance back at the couple we just fixed. They sit, gazing into each other's eyes, oblivious to the outside world. They look very happy, as if they are seeing each other for the first time. Perhaps they are.

We lean side by side, backs against the side wall of the café, breathless and laughing.

"So where to next, Hairy?" I ask, not wanting to gloat too much. I can't help feeling a little bit smug, though. This padlock lark seems like a bloody breeze. "Where do we find the next padlock?"

"We must look in places where couples might meet. Where lovers might go to find something they have lost." Any hint of laughter is gone from his face, and he is all business-like again.

"Are there many places like that around here?" If I sound doubtful, it's because I am. I mean, how many places like that can there be? "Are we going to spend the entire forty-eight hours in bloody cafés? I don't think I can drink anymore coffee. I'm still buzzing."

Lucien is staring at me as if I've just dribbled down my chin. "What?" I scowl.

"Mon cheri, we are in Paris," he tells me slowly, as if explaining to a child. "This is the most romantic city in the world. There are hundreds of places like that, and none of them are cafés."

"Really?" I am a little more optimistic in view of his enthusiasm. "So what are we waiting for, Hairy? Let's go."

Chapter 5: Locked in the Aisle

Of all the possible places we could go in this supposedly very romantic city, Lucien leads me into a shop. I thought we were looking for places where lovers would go. This doesn't seem very romantic, but what do I know?

"We're in a shop, Hairy. What's romantic about this?"

Lucien regards me with his hands on his hips.

I have to admit I do find his little displays of irritability quite funny, and—something else I don't understand—whatever! I fight the urge to snort every time he looks at me all narrow-eyed and full of hell.

"When was the last time you were inside a shop, Sol?"

"Erm...never." I feel a little sheepish, really.

"Well, then, let me find the couples, and you can help me fix them."

Ooh! He sounds a bit snippy.

"So I'm just supposed to trot along behind, like a good little troll, am I?" I grunt, looking around at the products on the shelves. I don't have a clue what any of them are. I can't read, and if the pictures on the labels are anything to go by, they all contain human babies. I pick one up and examine it closely, giving it a shake. "Since when did humans become cannibals?" I ask, sniffing the package dubiously. It smells funny but not unpleasant. I curl my nose anyway.

"Sol!" Lucien takes the packet from me with a huff of frustration and places it back on the shelf. "They are baby wipes."

"Urgh!" I make a face of disgust. "Why would anyone want to make wipes out of babies?"

"They aren't made out of babies, they are *for* babies." Lucien pulls me along the aisle, his eyes darting from side to side, as if he's hot on the trail of—something.

"Well, 'ow the 'ell was I supposed to know?" He does remember I can't read, doesn't he?

"Can you really not read?" He stops and looks at me with his head tipped to one side. It's kind of cute when he does that.

"No!" I snap. I indicate my eyes, get distracted by my human fingers, and then focus on what I was saying. "Troll eyes, they don't see the words right." And I never ever bothered to try learning to read, but he doesn't need to know that. Although he probably already realises that I'm lazy as well as stupid.

"Maybe you need glasses." Lucien regards me thoughtfully and then turns away, going back to his search. He peeks around a corner.

"What would I do wiv a pair of glasses, Hairy?" I snort. "They'd never fit under my monobrow."

Lucien snorts softly and places a finger over his lips.

"Shush!" He beckons for me to peek around the corner, too.

I do so, leaning over him easily, my chin almost rests on the top of his head. His back feels warm where it presses against my stomach. He really is quite tiny compared to me, but in this position, we kind of fit together well. It's doing things to my insides I don't quite understand. I feel this overwhelming urge to wrap my arm around him and pull him in tight.

"Concentrate, Sol," Lucien snaps. "The couple at the end of the next aisle. They are our next love lock."

I am intrigued about how he can sense it. I'm also intrigued that he smells slightly similar to those baby wipes I was just sniffing. No, it isn't an unpleasant scent at all.

To distract myself, I observe the couple. They are walking, seemingly aimlessly, down opposite sides of the aisle, dropping things listlessly into their wire mesh shopping baskets. Shopping's changed a bit since I last watched it. It doesn't look like we're going to find a moment here at all. They look positively miserable.

"'Ow do you know it's them, then?"

"I just know." He sighs impatiently. "Now, take my hand and close your eyes." He offers his hand back, and I take it, wondering what everyone around us will make of our position and the fact we have our eyes closed. Lucien nudges me with his backside. "No one can see us, Sol."

I forgot that he can hear my thoughts when we touch. I frown.

"'Ow do you mean, they can't see us?"

"Humans only see us if we wish them to. Right now, they cannot, because we do not."

"'Ow does that work, then? I never knew we could do that." If I had known, I could've been exploring this bloody city at will, instead of hiding away for centuries. "'Ow d'ya do it, then?"

~Shush, Sol, for goodness' sake. I will answer your questions later. Let's get this lock fixed.

I blow out my cheeks then sigh and close my eyes. I immediately feel that floating sensation again. The only thing that stops me from panicking is the fact that Lucien is holding my hand. The blurring and the fuzzy edges don't even distract me this time, as I follow the silvery thread of Lucien's thoughts. They lead directly to the couple. This time, I find myself inside the man's mind.

~Oh my gawd. It's a bloody mess in here. All of his memories are covered in what I conclude is dust, as if they haven't been looked at for years. ~What's going on?

~Lives in the moment, this one does, Lucien tells me. ~Which makes finding the 'moment' we want, a little more difficult and a little more intense.

~What do you mean, intense?

~You'll see. Lucien's chuckle tickles me inside and makes me squirm ever so slightly.

He doesn't offer any further explanation, so I get on with my search.

Sure enough, tucked away behind the other memories is a shrivelled grey one. I'm beginning to see a pattern here.

~*I've found it, Lucien, I think.* The memory is rapidly deflating.

~*Quickly, look inside.*

I do. It's—ordinary. The memory is of a bookshelf. A hand lifts to take a book, and another pulls it in a different direction. The point of view changes, and I see a pair of eyes.

~*Is this it?*

I'm a little underwhelmed. He said it would be intense.

~*Yes... Oh!*

Lucien sighs. I can sense he is smiling.

I don't have time to ask why as I pull the memory forwards. Suddenly, there is a resounding click, but instead of throwing me back into my body, I stay, locked in the memory, too.

~*Lucien, what's going on?* I realise it isn't me that's keeping us here. ~*Oy, Hairy, wakey wakey. We need to get out.*

~*Oh, sorry.* Lucien seems to snap back to the here and now, and we are eventually pulled back into our bodies.

I feel like I'm still floating, though. My skin is all tingly, and my mouth is dry.

"What the 'ell 'appened there?"

"It was love at first sight, Sol." Lucien leans back against the shelves. He has a dreamy look in his eyes, and he's smiling wistfully. "Wasn't it beautiful?" He looks high on something.

"They was fightin' over a book." I curl my lip in confusion. "'Ow is that romantic?"

"Oh, but don't you see? They fell in love over that book." His blue eyes are bright, as if they are lit by an inner light. It makes me swallow hard.

"If you say so. Why do I feel so floaty?" I would rather not feel lighter than air, since it feels like I could float away any minute. Not a good feeling for a troll that doesn't like heights.

"I told you it may be a little more intense."

"Intense?" I steady myself by placing a hand on his shoulder, and the vertigo slowly settles. "Any more intense, and I think I might vomit."

"Urgh!" Lucien walks away abruptly, leaving me off balance because I was leaning on him. He throws his arms in the air "Zut Alors! Pourquoi moi?"

Lucien continues to mutter angrily in French as I follow him out of the shop. He is scowling and looks frustrated as hell. I want desperately to laugh, because he's like an angry little cat, all spitty and hissy. He's got fire, this one.

I don't like fairies, I never have, but then I've never spent any decent length of time in their company. This one, he's different somehow. As I fall into step with him, and he smiles up at me, his little rant over, I find I am beginning to like him. A lot.

That aside, we have just mended our second lock, and we've only been at it ten minutes. How many will we be able to do in forty-eight hours if we keep up this pace?

Chapter 6: Locked in the Park

L UCIEN PULLS ME along a busy boulevard, weaving in and out of the ever-increasing crowd, taking a seemingly random route. Except it isn't random; he moves with feverish purpose. I remember watching a dog hunting once. Lucien's behaviour reminds me very much of this. He has picked up a scent, and he is following it. Occasionally, he stops, sniffs the air, and then pulls me in another direction. I am totally captivated.

How does he know what he's looking for? And when are we going to catch up with his mark? We've kept up this blistering, nonstop pace for ten minutes now. I'm ready to collapse.

"Here!" Lucien stops so abruptly I hurtle into his back. I only just manage to stop him from falling by wrapping an arm around his slim waist.

Instead of pulling away from me, he snuggles in. His hand covers mine, holding it in place and pressing it flat against his firm stomach. He reaches back and catches my chin with warm, delicate fingers. Turning my head gently, he points.

"See, over there, in the park."

I follow his point of view and see people sitting on benches, people milling about, people basically everywhere, but nothing specific that catches my eye. I can't concentrate. I am the one that wrapped my arm around him, but he is the one holding me possessively.

"Where?" It's impossible to see what he is pointing out; the park is full. I have no idea if this is normal so early in the morning, but there are far too many people for me to pick out anyone specific.

"Don't just look with your eyes, Sol." Lucien encourages me. "You saw it in the café—you could sense something was wrong. Now do it again."

I try but give up with a growl of frustration.

"There are still too many people, Hairy." Couples, families, people walking dogs, people arguing—oh. "I see them!"

"Good." Lucien smiles brightly, nodding. "You found them quickly, although this is quite an obvious one."

"Cocky bastard," I mutter. He chuckles, and I feel the sound as well as hear it. His body vibrates against mine, since I still have my arm around him, pulling him close.

Instead of thinking about why he seems to like being so close, I turn my attention back to the couple. They are arguing loudly. Looks like two women. It's hard to tell. Women used to all wear skirts that covered their ankles. Now everyone seems to wear trousers, whether they're men or women. These two, they both have short hair, and they're wearing clothes similar to the ones I've got on, except, I suppose, the shape of their figures gives away their gender. Definitely female.

"Ready?" Lucien tips his head back to look at me, raising his eyebrows in question. I nod.

I close my eyes and feel our minds travel together, towards the arguing couple.

They're loud. Shouting at each other and not caring where they are or who hears.

~Bloody hell, they need their moment badly, Hairy.

Once again I feel rather than hear Lucien's chuckle.

~They can certainly shout. Be careful, Sol. There are a lot of angry thoughts inside their heads. Try to avoid them.

~What happens if I touch one of the angry thoughts?

~If you get caught in their emotion, you could bring it back out with you. Angry emotions can leave you in a bad mood for the rest of the day.

~'Bad mood' is my middle name, Lucien. I doubt you'd notice any difference, mate.

The sensation of his chuckle and his tiny hand squeezing mine travels along my line of thought. I feel it, not only physically, but mentally too. For a millisecond I am lost to it, then I shake off the distraction and focus.

~You are getting better at this.

I can feel my face heat up as I recall, in this position, Lucien is privy to everything I think and feel. He knows I can't get this body's libido under control. He must think I'm a right dunce.

~Not a dunce, just confused. Stuck in a shitty situation and doing as well—in fact, better than anyone expected.

~Better than expected? You can explain that one to me when we're done with this couple.

~It was not me that ever doubted you, Sol.

There's no time for Lucien to expand on that statement, because suddenly I'm caught up in a wave of anger. The woman whose mind I'm inside is just one tightly wound, sizzling ball of flame. Her anger makes my skin itch. Ouch!

Like before there are bubbles. I have no idea if this is something I've conjured up to help cope with the strangeness of being in someone else's mind, or if this is what a human mind actually looks like. It doesn't matter. It works, so I'm not gonna bugger about with it.

The bubbles of memory inside this mind are all burning hot and covered in spikes as I push my way through them. I've got thick skin. They feel hot, but they don't burn. The spikes are a different matter. It makes me worry for Lucien.

~I am fine, concentrate on finding their moment.

I get the impression Lucien is talking through gritted teeth, but when I try to search his mind he shuts me out.

~I said I'm fine, Sol.

Well, I'm sorry for being concerned. He didn't need to snap at me, bloody hell.

This is different from the first two. Those couples hadn't been speaking to each other. They hadn't even been looking at each other. There'd been no emotion, just indescribable loss. These two are going at it like the clappers, and I've got a ringside seat. I can hear everything they're saying to each other, and it ain't pretty.

~*Blimey, they're givin' it what for, ain't they?*

~*Sol!*

~*Sorry, but it's not often I get to listen to someone other than myself getting angry over nothing.*

~*So glad you're enjoying yourself, now FIND THAT MEMORY!*

I recoil from Lucien's anger. He shouted in my head. It stung!

I stop listening to the argument, but it continues to provide a background soundtrack to my search. Eventually, after pushing through increasingly more prickly and fiery hot bubbles, I find it.

~*Lucien, I've got it.*

~*Finally! I thought you'd take all day. Just my luck to get stuck with a slow-as-hell bloody troll. Now pull the stupid thing forward and let's get out of here.*

~*O-okay!*

What's got up his nose? And what does he mean 'stuck'? He told me he volunteered to work with me. Was he lying? Well sod him. I should've known he was just like all the others.

I pull the memory bubble forward, not even bothering to check inside to see if it's the right one. It was the only one there that was deflated and grey anyway. This thing's a doddle. I don't even know why I have to work with that carrot-topped, snippy, fluffy little shit.

There is a resounding clang as the lock slams shut. I'm pulled back into my body so roughly I fall backwards onto my arse, and because my arm is still wrapped tightly around him, I pull Lucien with me. He falls into my lap and immediately struggles to stand. I try to help him, but he swipes my hands away angrily.

"Get off me, for goodness' sake," he snaps, rolling to his knees then standing. He thrusts his hands onto his hips, and his eyes flash dangerously as he glares down at me. "Why do we always end up in a heap on the ground?" he demands.

I laugh. I can't help it, because the anger is so out of place. He's so small and delicate that when his temper flares it makes me chortle.

"Do you think this is funny, Sol?" He narrows his eyes, while I try to contain my amusement. "Did you do it on purpose?"

"No! I fell." I scowl now. "Bloody hell, Hairy. You should think yourself bloody lucky I was there to break your fall, otherwise you'd be the one flat on your arse in the dirt."

"None of this is a joke, Sol." He waves his hands around, his expression livid. "This is for your benefit, but I might as well be doing this on my own. Zut alors! Did you even look at the memory before you brought it forward? We could have been looking at completely different memories, for all you know."

I stand and brush myself off. "Don't you bloody snipe at me. Don't forget, I'm the amateur here, Fairy Boy. I don't 'ave a fuckin' clue what I'm doin'. And for your information, it was the only memory that wasn't surrounded by flames and bloody thorns. Whoever she was, I'm bloody glad I don't have to be locked in love with her for the rest of my life."

"I can think of worse fates." Lucien sneers at me, and I remember his cutting remark when we were still inside that couple's minds.

"And what do you mean, stuck with me? You said you asked to be my partner."

"Yes, I asked, but I regret it now." He turns and stalks off. "Stuck or not," he calls back, "another mistake like that, and you'll find yourself looking for another partner. And believe me, no one else will be as understanding as I have been."

I chase after him, full of confusion, anger and hurt. His words have wounded me, damn it. Is that because I'm stuck in this human body, with human emotions to boot? Or because I've allowed myself to open up to him in a way I've never opened to anyone? I let him in and now I'm vulnerable. I have to put a stop to that.

"If you feel so strongly about it, Fairy, then why don't you just leave me alone and go off and find some other fairy stuff to do?"

He stops and takes a slow, angry breath, pinching the bridge of his prissy little nose.

"Let me try and explain this to you in simple terms that a stupid, thick-skulled troll might understand." I glare at him as he continues. "There is no other *fairy stuff* to do today, Sol, because someone—I don't think I have to name names here— did something so fucking selfish that everyone else has to spend their precious time running around picking up the damn pieces. I can't go and find anything else to do, because this is the only thing *ANYONE* is doing today. Unfortunately for me, no matter how much I might want to drop you like a lead weight, there won't be a change of partner, because no one wants to work with a big, fat, smelly, hairy *TROLL*."

After spitting those last words in my face, he turns on his heel and storms off again, leaving me stunned and speechless. All the things he's said since this began, all the ways that he made me feel he was different—that he wanted to get to know me, that he saw more than the black matted fur and sloping monobrow—it was all just words. To what end, though? Why would he be so nice and not mean it? How did I not see he wasn't being completely genuine with me?

I'm angry with myself for trusting him, for allowing myself to set him apart from the others.

"That's right. Storm off like the little prissy diva that you are," I shout after him. "Bloody fairies, you're all the same. Judge me on my looks, and all those damn stories that *aren't even bloody true*. Not one of you thought to ask me about any of it. None of you even bothered to ask my name. I was here long before any of your lot turned up, with all your bloody bureaucratic claptrap. Go on, bugger off. I can do this on my own, you bloody piece of fairy fluff."

I instantly regret what I've just shouted, but before I can apologise and catch Lucien up, he disappears. What the fuck? He left me.

"Lucien!" I shout. It's no good. He could be anywhere now, and as I look around in panic, I realise I could be anywhere too, because I don't have a damn clue where the fuck I am.

"Lucien! Come back here, you bloody bastard," I yell into thin air.

"Monsieur!" A man regards me with shock. "There are children present. Etre conscient des enfants, monsieur, s'il vous plaît."

I glare down at him and growl. "Oh shut yer cakehole," I hiss at him. He swallows and backsteps, gibbering in French.

I don't pay him any more attention and try to get my bearings. I can't believe Lucien would just leave me like that. If I backtrack, then I can probably find my way back to the river. I'll be okay once I'm there. Frantically, I look around for the gate we used to enter the park. There are several.

Then I spot him. A flash of red hair disappearing out of a gate across the other side of the park. He didn't go that far, then.

I take off in hot pursuit.

As I run, I wonder what brought on Lucien's outburst. All those things he said, they hurt, but despite the anger with which they were spoken, my gut tells me he didn't mean them. All the things he's said before that? Now they were genuine. He wants to help me, he asked to be assigned to me as my partner. I'm sure all of that was true. Why would he say such hurtful things now?

"Oh bloody hell, Sol, ye stupid great arse," I berate myself, pulling at my hair.

Of course it wasn't him saying all those things. It was the emotions from that other couple. It has to be. He told me himself.

You could end up bringing the emotions back out with you. I might not know him all that well, but my gut is telling me everything before just now was completely true. The words he's just spoken, they were the lies, brought on by the anger he absorbed whilst searching inside that angry woman's head.

And now he's gone off in a fit of rage that's not his own. What'll happen when he realises what he's done? I can imagine he'll be absolutely mortified. I have to find him.

"Lucien!" I shout as I run to the park gate where I saw him last.

I find myself on a busy boulevard. This is ridiculous. How many bloody people live in this damn city anyway? And the noise. It's worse here than on my bridge. Car engines revving, horns honking, everyone shouting angrily at everyone else, including me, because I'm in their way as I stand and try to seek out Lucien in the crowd.

He's had a head start, and he's so bloody tiny I'll never see him from ground level. I can't even rely on my sense of smell, because no matter how many times Lucien tells me I am still a troll locked inside a human body, I can't get used to smelling stuff through this skinny human nose. There's only one thing for it. I look to my side and see a lamppost, with a rubbish bin beside it.

Swallowing hard against bile, because even this height is too much for me, I step onto the bin and hold the lamppost for balance. From this angle, once my head has stopped swimming and my eyes are back in focus, I can see down into the crowd.

"Lucien! Hairy!" My shout turns heads. Everyone glances at me and then looks away with disinterest, as if they see a troll shouting and hanging from a lamppost every day.

"Monsieur, vous ne pouvez pas rester là," a deep voice with a tone of authority calls up to me from the ground. "Descendez à la fois."

"You what?" I glance down and see a man dressed in some sort of official looking garb: dark pants and light-blue shirt with silver numbers on his lapels. He's wearing a hat that makes me want to laugh, because it looks like he's got a hat box stuck on top of his head. His expression is very serious, though, and I think he's asking me to get down.

What was it that Lucien said? Humans only see us if we want them to? Well, I don't want to be seen by this guy or anyone right now.

"Zut alors. Où est il? Où est-il allé?" The man looks about him in confusion and fear, and he looks right through me as if I'm no longer there.

Well, what do you know? It works? Ha!

I ignore the man's shouts and go back to my search. Am I too late? Has Lucien disappeared down another street and out of sight? Just when I'm about to give up, I spot him. He's hard to miss, really, with his flaming auburn hair, like a thousand sunsets sitting on top of his head.

"Lucien!" I shout, but I know there's no way he can possibly hear me above all this noise. He's a good way ahead of me. I'm just in time to see him turn a corner and disappear again.

I jump down from the bin, ready to give chase but grab hold of the lamppost instead. Bloody hell! My knees almost buckle as a wave of dizziness, that has nothing to do with the height, washes over me. What's this new hell?

Is it linked to that couple as well? I don't know, but if Lucien is feeling only half as bad as I am right now, he'll surely be on his knees without me there to break his fall. My need to find him increases alarmingly.

I edge around the crowd that has gathered about the now hyperventilating official with the funny hat. He gestures wildly at the lamppost and covers his face with his hands as onlookers try to comfort him. I feel a bit bad that I've caused him distress, but finding Lucien is more important right now.

No time to think about the protective instinct this situation has invoked. Instead, I run.

Now that I can't be seen, it is far easier to manoeuvre through the crowds. They all assume the ones pushing them are someone else and not an invisible troll-turned-human. That's just as well, since, even when I wasn't running full pelt through the crowd, I attracted attention. Even as a human, I appear to tower above almost everybody else.

At the corner, I stop to catch my breath. Trolls aren't made for running any distance—or running at all, for that matter.

The street Lucien turned down is much smaller and far less crowded. Pushing past only a few dilly dalliers on the corner, I find the rest of the street relatively empty. There is no sign of Lucien, though. Where did he go now?

"Lucien!" I shout, hoping he can hear me when I'm in stealth mode. I don't have any idea how this even works. "Lucien!"

My voice echoes off the tall buildings, distorting it and making it difficult for me to hear if there is a reply.

I sniff the air. Here, there isn't so much to interfere with my sense of smell, like overpowering perfume, cologne and feet. Why do human feet smell so bad? I sniff again. I can detect a hint of…whatever it is that Lucien smells of. Definitely not feet. I follow the scent. There's an alley, halfway along the road.

Sure enough, he's there, standing just inside the entrance to the alley. He is standing with his back to me, his shoulder leaning against the wall, his head down. I can almost taste the relief at seeing him, but he's led me a merry dance, the bastard. How could he leave me stranded like that?

As I open my mouth to speak, my angry words are bitten back by a noise I'm not familiar with. I take a step closer, and I register what it is. A sob. Lucien is crying.

My heart feels like a rock in my chest as I watch his shoulders heave. I don't know why he's upset. Maybe it's because of what he said, or maybe it's just the fallout from such strong emotions leaving his body, but I do know I can't watch him cry and do nothing.

I close the gap and gently, tentatively place my hands on his shoulders.

"Lucien?" I'm awkward and clumsy and no fucking good at anything like this.

He tenses at my touch, and I think he's going to pull away, but he doesn't—the exact opposite, in fact. He turns, and I find my arms are suddenly full of sobbing fairy, his face buried in my shirt.

Awkwardness increases tenfold, as I wonder where the hell to put my hands. My arms are already wrapped around him. They went there of their own accord. My hands eventually settle on his back, stroking gently as I murmur softly to him.

"Alrigh', Hairy, there, there." Shit, how lame does that sound? I really am no good at this.

"I'm sorry, Sol. So sorry." Lucien sobs.

His hands have snaked up my back, and they cling to my shirt like he's afraid I'll leave. Like I have anywhere else to be right now, like I'd want to be anywhere else.

"I did not mean anything I said to you. And I shouldn't have left you alone in that park. Ce fut impardonnable." The words tumble out of his mouth, accented by sobs and hiccoughs.

"Don't you worry about it," I murmur, wondering where the hell I've been hiding this gentle side all my life. "Water under the bridge, mate. Water under the bridge."

It takes a few more minutes for his sobs to slow and eventually stop. I hold him through it, not feeling that inclined to let him go.

"What happened back there, Hairy? Was it that couple's emotions? Did you touch too many angry, spikey bubbles?"

He nods, sniffing and wiping his nose with a delicate lace handkerchief. "They were all packed so tightly, I could not help but touch them."

"You all right now?" I hook my thumb beneath his chin, and he smiles up at me.

He nods again and then pulls away, leaning back against the wall. I do the same, our arms almost touching but not quite. I can't help feeling a bit disappointed that he's moved, since I quite liked the way it felt when I held him.

I think I'm turning soft.

"How come it did not affect you?" Lucien tips his head back so he can see my face.

I shrug.

"'Ow do you know it didn't?" I smirk, and he snorts, nudging me gently. I frown as I think it all through. "It did a little, I think, but not as much as you. I guess I've got thicker skin."

"You may be right there, Sol."

"What do you mean?" I frown at him.

"I mean that some of us are more susceptible to other's emotions, like a sponge absorbing water. You, on the other hand, may be a little more water-resistant."

"No idea what you're talking about, Hairy, but I'm just a stupid, hairy, ugly troll, so I defer to your superior intellect."

Lucien buries his face in his hands with a groan. "You have to believe me. I did not mean any of that." He looks up into my eyes, stepping around so that he's facing me. "I don't think you are stupid. I happen to like that you're hairy, and you are definitely not ugly."

His words make me feel quite good, but I can't think they mean anything, really. I chuckle, looking down at myself.

"I'm not ugly like this, maybe."

"Not in any form." Lucien's smile is warm, and, I don't know, because no one's ever smiled at me like that before, but there's something that looks like affection in his eyes.

He doesn't hate me. He doesn't feel stuck with me. I still have no idea why he wants to help me so badly, except he says he wants to right a terrible wrong, whatever that means.

"Come on, Sol, let's get back to work." Lucien pushes himself away from the wall.

As I watch him, it's as if I'm seeing him clearly for the first time, and what I see makes my heart miss several beats. His face is pale, and his eyes are red rimmed. That's because he was crying, but the dark circles and drawn cheeks aren't because of that. He looks absolutely exhausted. Is that just because of what we've done today? If so, then he must have been working harder than me, because nothing we did seemed very strenuous. Perhaps it's something else as well?

I blink and suddenly his cheeks are rosy again, and his skin is the complexion of peaches and cream. What the...? Did I just imagine all of that? What's going on here?

"Lucien." I reach out to him in concern, but he's turned and is walking back out of the alley.

"Come, Sol. We have work to do and no time to waste." He hitches his shoulders, as if shrugging me away. He doesn't turn to face me. I think he knows I saw. "I sensed others in the park, some that were not so emotionally charged. If we are quick, we can find them all."

I follow him with a jumble of confused thoughts in my head and a determination to keep a closer eye on this fairy.

Chapter 7: Locked on a Bench

L UCIEN'S HIDING THE fact that he looks like death warmed up with some sort of spell. It's none of my business, except it did shock me. I don't want this lock business to cause him any pain or make him ill.

I don't have time to think about it—or about when I stopped being a selfish old troll and started thinking of someone else instead of myself.

Lucien has us all over the park in search of couples to mend. Despite the fact he looked exhausted for the split second his guard was down, he seems to be driven, like one of those new-fangled car contraptions that rumble over my bridge, day in, day out.

By the time midday approaches, we have fixed twenty-four locks. I don't think that's bad going. I do think it's time for a rest, though.

I still can't work out how he's finding these locks, but I'm not going to knock it.

I continue to be completely and utterly underwhelmed by these 'moments' that are supposed to be so pivotal and crucial to sealing the bond between two humans in love.

So far, I have witnessed humans realising their undying love over laundry, wire mesh shopping baskets, a tatty old book, a crossword, a pair of worn-out shoes, a scarf, an umbrella and a squashed spider. It's tedious. For goodness' sake. I don't know much about romance, but I'd like to think I'd have a bit more imagination. I've come to the conclusion that humans are quite boring.

We are currently sitting on a bench, people watching. Lucien shifts restlessly beside me, mostly because I've made him sit here.

I might be tired after traipsing around this park fixing lost loves, but he must be exhausted. He's never stopped.

He clicks his tongue in frustration at the forced rest.

"We ain't shiftin', Hairy, so you can stop all that shufflin' around." I lean back on the bench, folding my arms across my chest, just so he gets the message that I will not be changing my mind.

"But we need to move around, Sol. We should be in amongst the crowds to find broken couples," he grumbles beside me, but he doesn't try to get up.

"If we sit here long enough, the crowds will pass us. We can search just as well from this bench. I ain't moving another inch. My feet are bloody killing me." They're not, but he doesn't need to know that. He thinks it's because I'm not used to walking around on human feet, and it was a good enough ruse to get him to sit. "I haven't walked around this much since the Romans left a thousand years ago."

He snorts and regards me with sparkling eyes. "Truly?" He sounds dubious, but I can also see wonder in his expression. "You have lived through so many ages, Sol. You must have a great many stories to tell."

"Not really." I stare off into the distance. "I slept through most of it, and when I was awake—when I wasn't being chased around with pitchforks or persecuted by goats—I spent most of my time underneath, or in the vicinity of my bridge. This—" I wave my hands about me "—is the furthest I've been from my bridge… erm…ever, actually."

"That is quite sad, Sol. Because of others' ignorance, there is so much you have missed." Lucien lays a hand on my arm, and I fight the urge to jump a mile, because it still sends shocks and tingles through my entire body every time he touches me. Sometimes, I wonder if it wouldn't be better to keep in physical contact all the time; then the sensations might be lessened.

I take his hand from my arm and hold it in my lap.

"I don't feel like I've missed anything, Hairy. I'm not a very adventurous troll. In fact, bridge trolls as a species aren't all that adventurous. We prefer to stay close to our bridges."

His hand feels tiny in mine, and warm, and soft. I need to keep talking.

"What about fairies? I expect you get about a bit more because of the wings thing." I point at his back and then inwardly groan, because it's not like he doesn't know where his bloody wings are.

Lucien shifts his shoulders a little but doesn't answer. When I chance a sideways glance at him, he is staring down at his hand in mine. Slowly, he turns it, so our palms are facing. His fingers link through mine, and my breath catches in my throat. Maybe holding his hand wasn't such a good idea, because now I have tingling shocks and I can't breathe. I pull away, and Lucien gives a small huff, narrowing his eyes before gasping and turning his head to stare over to the other side of the park.

"There, over at that bench." He points, and we are back in business, looking to fix our twenty-fifth lock.

The couple sit close to each other, looking as if they are simply resting together on the bench. I sense the same from them as I have from all the others. There is something missing. They look lost. They don't look as desperately unhappy as the others, though. In fact, they are looking about them quite hopefully.

"Great work, Hairy." I slap him on the back slightly awkwardly because of the hand-holding thing.

His smile tells me everything is fine.

"Best get started then." Lucien holds out his hand with raised eyebrows.

Great. Having just pulled my hand from his, I now have to hold it again.

~Feels a little different this one, Hairy.

I can't put my finger on it, but this couple don't seem as unaware of their situation as the others.

~They have been together longer, Sol. Their moment happened a long time ago for them but is still so very precious that they feel the *loss of it keenly. They are very perceptive. We must tread carefully. They may sense our presence.*

~Blimey. What happens if they don't want us in there?

~I think we need to ask their permission before we go in.

~How?

"We must go and speak to them, Sol." Lucien looks troubled. "It means revealing who we are and what we are doing. They may believe us, or they may think we're crackpots and tell us to get lost."

"Great." I bite my lip.

Telling them who we are could be a problem if these people have an issue with trolls. What if they turn us away because I'm a troll? I am wracked with self-doubt as Lucien leads me by the hand towards the bench where the couple are sitting.

"Bonjour, madame, monsieur," Lucien greets them cheerily. "Je m'appelle Lucien. Ceci est mon petit ami, Sol. Pouvons nous asseoir ici?"

The couple smile up at us with a look of anticipation, and the man indicates the space beside him. Lucien pulls me down with him. I don't speak much French at all, but did he just call me his 'little friend'? I want to laugh, because I am far from little, and the fact that he called me that is probably why the couple are now regarding me with slight amusement.

Well, at least that seemed to cheer them up.

Lucien continues to converse with the man in French, while the woman regards me with curiosity. I flick my eyebrows at her, feeling a little awkward. When she winks at me, I feel my cheeks heat up, and I am suddenly very glad that Lucien is holding my hand, because at least she doesn't think I'm available for flirting or anything.

I swallow nervously when she stands up and moves along the bench to sit beside me.

"I have to say, you don't look like a troll." She smiles, her eyes travelling up and down my body appreciatively. "At least, not the trolls I remember reading about in my childhood."

Her accent is rich and lyrical, like Lucien's. I stare at her for various reasons. She knows I'm a troll, and she's not running for her life. I suppose Lucien told them. She doesn't seem fazed one little bit, and neither does her partner.

"You shouldn't believe fairy tales, lady," I grumble at her. "They're told by parents to scare their kids."

"I doubt you would scare anyone." The woman gives me such a genuine, friendly smile I'm a little taken aback.

I frown, but I can feel myself relaxing. "You ain't exactly catching me at my best."

She chuckles. "No. I can imagine you look very different when you aren't trying to look human."

I regard her with a frown. "How come you ain't callin' us cranks and tellin' us to bugger off?"

"Sol, be nice," Lucien mutters from behind me. I huff and roll my eyes. The woman laughs.

"I am Juliette. My husband's name is Jean." She offers a delicate hand, and I stare down at it, because touching skin to skin feels like hot pokers are being shoved through every part of my body at once. It's not unpleasant, just intense. I take her hand anyway and—nothing happens. Well that's a first, but then, she is the first human I have ever touched. The reaction I get when I touch Lucien must be because he's a fairy. Must be to do with all that fairy dust and glitter.

"Nice to meet ya, Juliette." I make an attempt at a smile, hoping it isn't too creepy or out of place on my human face.

"Lucien told me what you are here to do." Juliette's eyes reveal an inner sadness that she was merely hiding well. "I have to admit, this is the reason we came here today. When Jean and I woke this morning, we knew something was wrong. We have been married for fifty years, and this is the first morning that my husband has not brought me a cup of tea, and the first morning I forgot to tell him I love him." She grasps both my hands in hers—no mean feat, because she's smaller than Lucien. She holds them tightly, her eyes searching my face. "The news is all over the city, that the locks have been taken away. Everyone thinks it was a city council order, but we knew that could not have happened overnight. We knew the fairies had a hand in it somewhere and would be trying to sort it out. You are here to help us, yes?"

I nod, because I suddenly feel a lump forming in my throat the size of a river boulder. This woman's calm dignity in the face of desperation has touched me more than any of the other locks we have fixed this morning.

"Please, Sol. Help us find our moment. It is so precious, but it is lost. We have spoken of it every day since it happened, except for today. We knew something terrible had happened. Thank God you are here. We have waited all morning for Les Fée to find us."

"Well, we've found you now, Juliette. We'll help, I promise."

This is all a bit overwhelming, because for the first time since this thing started, it feels personal. Meeting this couple has suddenly hammered home just what an impact my actions have had on the people in this city and further afield. What about those couples? Who's helping them? Bloody hell. I understand Lucien's distress when I first cast the spell, and his absolute focus on finding and fixing as many locks as possible, to the detriment of everything else.

What these two human beings feel for each other isn't tedious. It doesn't matter whether their moment is incredibly moving or mind-numbingly boring, it's their moment and they lost it because of me. They deserve to get it back.

~*Oh my gawd, Lucien, we 'ave to 'elp these people. We have to help all of them.*

Lucien turns to face me and smiles, squeezing my hand, which sends familiar shocks through my body.

~*Finally you see. It is a start.*

Chapter 8: Locked in an Alley

A MILLION 'WHAT IFS' are running through my head. The main one involves that last couple. Meeting them and seeing it all from their point of view has finally hit home what an impact my one reckless act is having everywhere. And on everyone.

What if we hadn't found Juliette and Jean in time? What if we'd just walked straight past them while they waited so patiently for someone to find them? What if we'd never found the memory of their moment?

They had such faith that we would be able to help them. Such trust in our abilities. But they are the lucky ones. They knew what was happening. How many others are like them? How many others are hurting and don't have a fucking clue why? I don't think I can cope with this. I think my heart is going to break in two.

"What would've happened to that couple if we hadn't gotten to them in time?" I ask Lucien as we walk back through the park.

"Their moment would have been lost forever." He sounds tired and sad. "We would not have been able to reseal their lock."

I swallow against the lump that still sits in my throat.

"Would they have stayed together?"

He shrugs. "I do not know. They have been together for a long time. They have plenty of other memories to remind them why they fell in love. They would have mourned the loss of their moment though, because they knew it had been taken from them."

By me. I took it from them. The knowledge is horrendous. The scale of this thing is horrific. How many lives? How many loves have I ruined today?

"How many locks were on my bridge?" I turn to Lucien, feeling panic rising from my belly.

"I do not know." He gives me a startled look. "I don't think anyone ever counted them. Thousands, hundreds of thousands. A million maybe?"

"Oh my god." I start to shiver. "And I broke them all because I wanted a better night's sleep. How fucking selfish is that?" I am finding it hard to breathe, and I feel dizzy and faint.

"Sol?" Lucien is suddenly holding me up. "Zut Alors."

We've exited the park and we're back on the street. He leads me around a corner into an alley, where he urges me to sit. I'm hyperventilating by the time we get there.

"Sol!" He holds my face in his hands, tipping it so I am forced to look up at him. "Take deep breaths, mon cheri."

"All those people." I gasp. "At least that last couple had a bit of an insight into what was happening. The others, though." I sob, and hold my hand over my mouth in horror. "Bloody hell, Lucien. The others we fixed, they didn't have a clue what was happening." I stand and start to pace. "A million locks?" I look at Lucien, who nods as he watches me carefully. "And we've only done twenty-five. How can we possibly fix them all?"

"We don't have to fix them all, Sol, just one hundred. You know that. The other teams have similar targets. With everyone working together, the locks will be fixed in no time. Do not forget, a lot of those locks were no longer active." Lucien's voice is calm as he tries to soothe and reassure me, but it's no good.

I'm beyond where listening to a soothing voice will help. I'm in full-scale panic mode.

"What if we don't get to all of them in time?"

"I do not know." I can see Lucien has the same concerns; he's just better at hiding them. "Some of the couples may not stay together even if we do find them all. Human love can be very fickle."

"All this stress over nuffin'?" I gasp and gape at him. "Chasin' around fixing the things, only for bloody humans to mess up anyway. Why are we even bovverin'?"

"You know why, Sol. You have seen why. You have felt it. There is such anger when love is lost. The longer we leave it, the more anger there will be. Fickle or not, the world cannot live without love. We must do everything we can to try to fix these locks."

"Fucking hell, Lucien. This is all my fault. I was so fucking selfish. How can you even bear to look at me?"

"No one ever tried to explain what the locks meant." Lucien reaches out to me. "Sol, you did cast the spell, but you were not to know what impact that act would have."

"Juliette, she said she'd heard the locks 'ad all disappeared."

"Yes." Lucien nods. "No doubt the entire city knows by now. Something like that is difficult to hide and there was no point casting any illusion spells until the furore died down. Everyone was needed to mend locks."

"Oh my god." I lean back against the wall and hide my face in my hands. "If the entire city knows, that's it. I can't go back to my bridge. Everyone'll know I'm the one that caused the problem in the first place."

"No one knows it was you," Lucien assures me gently. "Madame Queen will not have broadcast that information to the other teams."

"No? But it's only a matter of time, isn't it?" I gasp in short, panicky breaths. "Your lot might be bureaucratic twats, but they ain't stupid. They'll put two and two together. Shit. It'll be like the goat incident all over again, except worse, because this time it is my fault, all of it."

"Sol. You need to calm down." Lucien's tone is a little firmer.

"Calm down?" I pull at my hair as I turn away from him. "How can I calm down? All those people whose lives I've ruined,"

I repeat in a high-pitched, hoarse tone. The alley is closing in around me. There's not enough air. "This'll just be another story parents can use to frighten their kids. I'll be run out of town, and the world will hate me because I took away all the love for the sake of a fucking good night's slee…mmmm!"

Suddenly I can't breathe for another reason. Lucien's lips are pressed against mine, and my brain is about to explode with sensation. My eyes are wide, and I think I might have squeaked.

His hands grasp the front of my shirt, pulling me down as he stands on his tiptoes to reach me. His lips feel warm and soft against mine. Slowly my eyes close, and I lose myself to the kiss.

I've never been kissed, but my body somehow knows what to do. My hands grab at his shoulders to pull him closer. My arms wrap around him and tighten the hold, until his body is pressed so firmly against mine there's a danger we might merge into one.

The sensations are overwhelming. That tingling I feel every time Lucien touches me increases to a crescendo. I can't process it at all, except I know it's halted my panic attack. His kiss is the perfect distraction.

He pulls away but does not break away completely. He searches my face with his luminescent eyes and caresses my cheek, brushing his thumb across my bottom lip as I watch him with startled wonder.

Lucien just kissed me. Lucien just kissed *me?*

"Are we good now?" he asks gently.

All I can do is nod. My brain is stunned. I'm sure my lips will tingle forever. I cannot form a word. I am struck dumb. If anyone asked my name right now, I doubt I would even remember that.

"Shall we go?" Lucien steps away and my body follows his movement, not wanting to lose the warmth of him against me. "Come, Sol. We have work to do."

Lucien walks from the alley like nothing happened, and I follow like a little lost puppy.

What the hell?

Chapter 9: Locked in a Puzzle

"Lucien!" I call as I try to catch him up. He's striding along a wide, tree-lined boulevard at break-neck speed. I'm not so quick, mostly because my legs have turned to jelly, and the rest of my bones to liquid after that kiss. I eventually catch up and fall into step beside him.

"Lucien, what the 'ell was that back there?" I gesture back towards the alley.

"I would have thought that was obvious, Sol." He doesn't meet my eye as he speaks, sounding a little distracted because he is doing that searching thing he does. "It was a kiss."

"I know it was a bloody kiss, Hairy." I sneer at him. "Do you think I don't know what a kiss is?"

He stops to regard me with raised eyebrows and his head tips to one side.

"Why did you ask what it was then, if you already knew?"

Ooh! He's so bloody annoying. I'd quite like to push him up against the nearest wall and kiss him again, just to take that smug look off his face, but I don't know how he'd react. He kissed me, not the other way around. It was to distract me, not for any other reason.

"I asked because I don't know why you would even want to kiss me."

Lucien narrows his eyes and places his hands on his hips. "Then you are blind." He sniffs, tosses his hair and storms off along the pavement. "And stupid," he calls back with another, angry flick of his hair.

"Oy!" I have to run to catch up with him again. "What do you mean, I'm blind?"

"I notice you do not deny that you are stupid." Lucien continues to walk while I stop and try to catch up on what's just been said.

Maybe I am stupid, because I can't for the life of me work out why he'd ever want to kiss a troll.

"Monsieur? Êtes-vous perdu?" A young woman asks me as I just stand there, staring after Lucien.

She's with a group of other young women, all smiling at me and giggling. I must look completely lost and ridiculous to them. Lost and totally out of place.

"Non, merci, mademoiselles." I thank her and her friends and take off after Lucien with another puzzle to ponder. When did I learn to speak French?

"Au revoir, monsieur."

I look back, and they are all waving and batting their eyes. I flash them a broad grin, and they all giggle again. Well that's provided some light relief. Having people admire me, instead of run screaming for their life, is a bit of a novelty really.

They were all pretty enough, I suppose, but a little young for me—by about twenty centuries—and not a patch on my fairy.

My fairy? What the hell? He ain't my fairy any more than I'm his troll.

"Sol. Hurry up." Lucien is waiting for me, tapping his foot and looking impatient. "When you have quite finished flirting with the entire female population of Paris, we have locks to fix."

"That's a bit of an exaggeration, Hairy. It was just a bunch of girls…" I stop and raise my eyebrows. I don't know about stupid, but I am being a bit slow on the uptake here. "Wait a minute. Are you jealous?" I laugh at the ridiculousness of that statement. What could he possibly have to be jealous of?

"Non!" He scowls and turns away, but I see his blush. His pale complexion can't hide it. "Come, we are wasting time." He sets off again, grabbing my hand so I don't lag behind, and also, I think, so I don't get accosted by any more pretty young women.

Well, okay. I think I might be his troll. Just a little bit.

"Where are we goin'?" I ask, as we pass another park full of people. I wonder why there aren't any locks to fix in there.

All irritation and impatience has gone from Lucien's expression, and he is back in business. He has that distant look in his eyes again. I've come to recognise it as Lucien on the trail of broken locks. All I can do is follow him. I'm a bit of a useless lump during this stage of the process. I'm not much better in the next stage either. I feel like I'm flying by the seat of my pants most of the time.

"I could not do this without you." Lucien squeezes my hand in support.

"You wouldn't 'ave to do it at all, if it weren't for me." I huff sullenly.

I won't allow myself to get so worked up again. Last time, Lucien was forced to kiss me to shut me up. Goodness knows what he'll do next.

"Try it, and see." Lucien flicks his eyebrows, and I laugh. I wish I could read his thoughts so easily.

"That will come, with time, mon cheri." He flicks his eyebrows again. "Practice makes perfect." Somehow I get the feeling he isn't just talking about the fixing of locks.

Is he flirting with me? I wouldn't know, since, apart from those girls just now, I've not had much experience of flirting, or interactions with anyone of any sort, for that matter. It's been a day full of firsts for me. Leaving my bridge, meeting humans, speaking French, flirting, kissing fairies, having someone look at me and not run a mile. This being human lark is certainly interesting.

The park we've passed is enormous. But we don't stop.

"Lucien, surely there were locks in there to fix." I frown as we walk down another wide boulevard and away from the park packed full of humans.

"There are other teams working in these parks," Lucien explains. "Urgh, this is so frustrating." He stops and stamps his foot. "Every time I find a lock, someone else gets there first. There are too many of us working here. We need to stop and rethink our strategy."

He pinches his nose as he tries, I assume, to think of where else to go.

My stomach gives an almighty growl. Lucien looks startled, and I bite my lip in embarrassment.

"Are you hungry, by any chance?" Lucien's eyes sparkle with mirth.

"Er, yeah, you could say that." I am mortified at my body's betrayal. How embarrassing. "The only thing we've had to eat today was those croissant things this morning, and before that, I hadn't eaten since before I went into hibernation."

"Zut Alors, Sol, please tell me you are joking." He gapes at me. "That was over a hundred and fifty years ago."

I give a helpless shrug. "What can I say? Trolls sleep a lot."

"But you also need to eat, mon cheri. Come." He takes my hand once more and leads me towards another stylish-looking pavement café. "We will take a break. Perhaps I can get in touch with other teams and see where they have not visited yet."

We're shown to a table by a waiter almost as tiny as Lucien, and this time, I try not to look or act too intimidating.

My mouth begins to water at the thought of food, any food. I don't have a clue what to have, because I'm sure my usual diet of rats and river weed isn't on the menu. To be honest, I didn't even realise I was hungry until my stomach gave the game away. I've been kind of distracted by everything else.

Lucien orders for us, mostly because I don't know what to have, but also because I can't read the menu. As we wait for our food, we discuss the lack of locks.

The atmosphere seems much brighter here. People are smiling and laughing, and generally they all look very happy.

"I suppose it's a positive thing that we aren't finding the locks so easily now." I try to be the optimist this time. "It means there are less to fix, right?"

"Perhaps you are right." Lucien doesn't sound convinced. "It means it will be harder to meet your target of one hundred."

I shrug. "I'm sure we'll find some somewhere."

It's only lunchtime. We have a day and a half left and seventy-five locks to fix. I'm sure we'll do it. I have every faith in my lovely little fairy.

Okay, I have to stop thinking like this.

"I have made a call to any teams working nearby." Lucien explains, oblivious to my inner ramblings. "They will let me know if there are any locks left in this area."

I try to locate other fairies out on the street but there are so many people passing the café, and I wouldn't know what they looked like anyway.

"Do you think they're doing it on purpose to stop me from fixing enough locks?"

Lucien gives me a sharp look.

"What makes you say that?" He frowns. "What would anyone gain by keeping you stuck in a human body and homeless?"

I shrug. "It was just a thought. Your Madame Queen, she said something about wanting to move me on years ago, but she was talked out of it."

"Yes." Lucien is still frowning. "By me."

"You?"

He nods absently, still looking about him, searching even now, when he's supposed to be taking a break.

"When humans first began placing locks onto your bridge, Madame Queen wanted to move you on, but you were hibernating. I did not think it would be fair to disturb you." He raises his eyebrows, and I roll my eyes at the implication of his words.

"The locks woke me up anyway," I grumble.

"I know." He sighs with what sounds like regret. "If I had known they would disturb you so much, I might have been able to do something about it when they first began to appear."

I'm surprised by his admission. He must have been around for well over two centuries, because I remember him trying to speak to me the last time I woke up. I'd had enough of fairy bureaucracy by then. I managed to do a disappearing act before he got anywhere near. I kind of wish I hadn't now. Things might have turned out differently.

"Exactly how long have you been hangin' around, Hairy?"

"I have watched over your bridge in its various guises, for three centuries, Sol." He looks uncomfortable, as if this is an admission of guilt and not an answer to my question. "Non!" he exclaims, slapping the table and cutting off any further questions I might have, like *why?* "I do not believe that anyone is trying to stop us from fixing locks. This is too important to everyone I have spoken to. We will just have to keep moving and find locks elsewhere. We should perhaps have stayed closer to the river anyway."

I agree with him there, but not because I think we might find more locks, just because then I'd know where the hell I was.

We sit in silence for a few moments. It gives me time to think about what he's just told me.

Why would he watch over my bridge for three centuries? Was he given the job? It must have been some sort of punishment. He can't have chosen such a tedious task. I mean, I was asleep for most of that time. He must have been bored out of his skull.

I also think about my, or rather, *our* task. In return for fixing one hundred locks, Madame Queen has apparently promised to restore me to my troll form. At least that was the message

Lucien gave me, and I have no reason to think he was lying. He said nothing about my continued residence beneath the bridge, though. I just took that condition for granted. I'm not so sure now. I'm not even sure I want to stay there, except I've got nowhere else to go. Perhaps there is, if she wanted to move me on once before. I can't help wondering where she'd move me on to.

"Even with the locks all gone from the bridge, do you think Madame Queen will let me stay? After the chaos I've caused?"

"I do not know." Lucien gives me a sad look. "She may give you the option to move if you wish."

"The option?" I frown. "I've never thought about living anywhere else. I never thought there even was an option."

But if there was, wouldn't it be better for everyone if I moved out of the city?

"Would you relocate, if you could? If you had somewhere else to go?" Lucien's voice is small, and he asks the question as if his entire world pivots around the answer I'm about to give.

"I don't know, Lucien." I shrug. "If I had a bridge somewhere quiet, somewhere there wasn't that many people, and there was no chance of a city being built around me as I slept, maybe. It's only a bridge, after all, and it's not much of a bridge either really. I don't have any other reason to stay in Paris."

"Oh." He looks away with a sigh. "Perhaps not."

He looks unhappy. Is it because of what I've said? I don't have any ties here, other than that bridge, or at least I didn't until today. Have I hurt his feelings? Did he think I would choose to stay for another reason? For him? His crestfallen expression tells me that is exactly what he was expecting.

I've never had a friend. Does he want to be my friend? Does he want more? I know he kissed me, but that didn't mean anything to him, did it? The more I think about it, the more I don't want this to end when my task has ended.

Whatever happens when tomorrow eventually comes around, maybe the friendship doesn't have to end. If I was to leave, maybe he could come with me. Would he want to? The only way I'll find that out is if I ask him.

I reach across the table and take his hands. He regards me with wide, blue eyes that are beautiful and precious and…

"Lucien…"

Before I can ask, our meal arrives. Lucien quickly pulls his hands from mine as the waiter places our food down in front of us.

He speaks in French, and Lucien answers, looking a little sad, or is he relieved? I can't tell.

Bloody hell, did that waiter just save me from making a monumental fool of myself? Why the hell would Lucien even consider coming with me anywhere? When this is over, I'll be a troll again. He doesn't want to be with a troll.

What kind of life could I offer him anyway? He lives in a beautiful riverside apartment. I live under a crumbling, smelly old bridge. That is always assuming I even have somewhere to live after all of this is finished, which is by no means carved in stone.

I watch him as he picks delicately at his food, lost in thought. Despite my dilemma, I'm a bit hungrier, and it takes all of my concentration not to shovel the lot into my mouth in one go.

Lucien gives me a distracted smile as I struggle with a knife and fork for the first time ever. Without comment or judgement, he takes the confounded implements from me, helps me hold them properly, and then goes back to pushing his food around on his plate.

Lucien is a puzzle to me. Every time I think I've learned something about him, there are a dozen more things I want to ask. Instead of asking, I study him. He's looking more tired and pale as the day goes on. I guess whatever spell he's been using to hide the dark circles beneath his eyes is beginning to wear off. We've been working hard all morning, and I feel tired, but not half as tired as he looks.

I guess he's been working harder than me. I wish I could do more, but I don't know what. I wish we could rest for longer, but I know he would never consider it. I wish he would tell me what's wrong with him, because I have this horrible feeling it isn't just tiredness. Most of all, I wish I could have asked him that question about coming with me before that waiter had brought our food. Perhaps that last one was for the best, though.

"Zut Alors," Lucien suddenly exclaims, startling me. He's looking out of the café and up at the sky.

"What?" I ask, trying to follow his gaze.

"Non." He shakes his head and looks dejectedly at the table. "C'est impossible."

"What?" I ask again, still looking out of the window, unable to see what might have made him exclaim so suddenly. "Have you found some locks to fix? Are they close?" I search his face in anticipation.

"Yes." He frowns, his blue eyes look troubled. "And no one has tried to search there yet. I sense there are dozens of locks to fix. But we cannot go, Sol." He shakes his head, seemingly resigned to the fact. "It is impossible."

I don't believe he's giving up that easily. "Why do you think it's impossible?"

Lucien takes hold of my chin and turns my head as he points up, and up, and up, high above the roofs of the tallest buildings on the other side of the wide boulevard. I see where he is pointing, and the food I have eaten so far begins to churn in my stomach.

"What the bloody 'ell is that?" I manage to squeak.

"That, mon cheri, is the Eiffel Tower."

Chapter 10: Locked in a Tower

Y OU HAVE GOT to be bloody joking, Hairy." We stand at the base of quite literally the tallest damn tower I have ever seen. "You are not seriously suggesting we climb that. I couldn't cope being three storeys up in your apartment. How am I gonna cope up there?"

"The broken locks are up there, Sol, and we are running out of time. I sense great despair. Have you forgotten Juliette and Jean?"

I narrow my eyes. Emotional blackmail is a bit below the belt for him, but it's bloody working. If I could save even one more couple like Juliette and Jean, I'd climb a mountain to do it. I'd climb to the bloody moon.

"Come on, Hairy. Let's get going."

He leads me past a queue of humans, towards a metal box packed with more humans. The smell of feet is overpowering. I screw up my nose and pull back.

"Sol!" Lucien's warning tone urges me on.

"Phew!" I hold my nose. "Why do human feet have to stink so bad?"

Lucien chuckles as he pushes me into the box and to the back wall, squeezing past humans, all standing shoulder to shoulder.

"You have human feet, or had you forgotten?" He grins up at me.

"Yeah, but mine don't smell."

"In your opinion." Lucien screws his nose up, and I narrow my eyes.

"Oy, shut it, Fairy Boy."

He just laughs harder, which makes me laugh, too. I stop when the metal box we're crammed into jerks slightly. Even though I can't see once the doors have slid shut, I can feel we are rising. I close my eyes and swallow against a wave of nausea. Lucien's arm slips around my waist.

"What is this thing anyway?" I ask out of the corner of my mouth. I can't turn because I'm pushed against the back wall, with Lucien tucked into my side, and shoulder to shoulder with everyone else.

"This is an elevator," Lucien whispers, his head leaning against my arm. "It will take us to the first platform. I did not think you would want to try climbing the stairs."

I swallow hard and pull at my collar as the walls close in around me.

"I don't know if this is better or worse."

~You'll be fine. Just think of the couples you will help. The good you will do.

Lucien's voice inside my head is clear as a bell and comforting. It calms me down.

~Whatever magic you're using, Lucien, it's working.

~No magic, mon cheri. Just distraction.

I chuckle and pull his arm tighter around me, linking my fingers with his. His touch sends shivers up and down my spine. The sensation that was unusual and confusing at first has become something I think I will miss terribly when we eventually finish this task tomorrow. I know I will find it difficult to say goodbye to him.

"Are there locks to fix in 'ere?" I still need more distraction as the elevator takes us higher and higher—oh, God—I need distraction bad.

"Perhaps, but we are too tightly packed in this contraption. There is danger of us touching the wrong mind, because we are in physical contact with so many at once." Lucien's voice sounds strained. I look down at him, and it seems he needs a distraction as much as I do.

"What's wrong?" All of my anxiety is pushed to the back of my mind in my concern for him. He has gone very pale.

"We are too close to them all, Sol. I sense all of their despair."
He closes his eyes. "Touch is not good. I don't—I can't…"

I don't even think, I wrap him in my arms, pulling him close.
My body serves as a barrier between him and the humans packed
around us.

"Better?"

He nods and slowly relaxes in my arms.

I glance about me. The humans packed in here with us are
all just standing there. Their expressions are blank, like they feel
nothing. The atmosphere is heavy with despair. I know what
Lucien means now when he said we were too close. I sense it too.

~*You must not think about it, Sol. Don't let it reach your heart.*
Lucien's voice is small and distant, like I'm losing him.

~*No, Lucien. Stay with me.*

~*Of course, mon amour. Je vais rester avec toi pour toujours.*

I don't know what he said, but it sounded nice. The words ring
in my head like a bell. I hold him closer. His body feels warm and
firm as he melts against me with a soft sigh. I can't help reacting.
I think of that kiss, and my body hardens.

"Sol!" Lucien breathes. He must feel the swell of my cock. I
can't hide it from him in these cramped conditions.

"Sorry." I release my hold on him but he pushes back against
me.

"Please don't stop." He pulls my arms back around him and
pushes his backside against my thigh.

"You don't mind touching me, I notice." I lean in and whisper
in his ear, feeling him tremble.

"I have never minded touching you, Sol," Lucien murmurs
back. His head tips to one side, giving me access to creamy
smooth skin.

My lips play across his neck. I feel the flutter of his pulse as
I press a soft kiss to his exposed neck. He's driving me bloody
crazy, and I don't know if this is a good idea, but I'll try anything
not to lose him to this despair around us.

"Er…Lucien?" I whisper against his skin.

"Oui?" He sounds out of breath.

"How did we manage to jump that queue just now?"

"We cannot be seen if we do not wish it, remember?"

"I remember. I just wanted to check we couldn't be seen before I did this."

I turn us both until he is pressed against the wall. With a gasp he turns to face me. He looks up at me with a challenge in his eyes, and I meet it. Taking his hands and holding them above his head, I bend to kiss him.

His arms wriggle free of my tentative hold and wrap around my neck, pulling me deeper into the kiss. His warm tongue finds mine.

~Sol.

Even his mental voice sounds breathless. It's like a sigh inside my head.

I press him harder against the wall, bending one knee to push between his legs. A delicious moan rumbles in his throat as he opens his legs to allow better access. I can feel how hard he is, and the kiss becomes heated as he rubs his groin against my thigh.

"Sol!" he sobs as our lips pull apart. I press a line of wet kisses along his jaw to his ear and then his neck, each one emphasised by a gasp or a sigh from him.

His face is flushed as I pull back, and his eyes are closed. Slowly he opens them to meet my gaze.

"What was that for?" he asks, his eyes sparkling with wonder.

"You needed a distraction, and so did I." I shrug, trying to act as nonchalantly as he did when he kissed me in the alley. "It worked a treat that first time."

He buries his face in my shirt, his forehead pressed against my chest as he giggles breathlessly.

"I can't believe we just made out in a crowded elevator."

"No one can see us, you said so. Seemed like a good idea at the time." I smile and hold him tight against me, smoothing my hand over his beautiful auburn curls.

"It was a very good idea, Sol." Lucien snuggles against my chest and I bury my face in his delicious hair, breathing in his unique scent.

I could do this forever. Lucien in my arms feels right, like he was meant to be there, like he should have been there long before now.

The spell is broken by a tinging noise and a voice announcing something in French.

"This is our stop, mon cheri," Lucien informs me with more than a hint of regret. He grabs my hand and pulls me from the elevator. "Oh, the view is amazing."

I try not to let the panic take over when I see how high we are, but there is nothing to be seen here but the view. I press my back against the nearest interior wall and slowly sink to the floor until I'm sitting, hugging my knees. We're so damn high, and this is only the first platform.

"Do we have to go all the way to the top?" I whimper as I take deep breaths to calm myself down.

Lucien makes a sympathetic noise and bends down to kiss my cheek.

"We only go all the way if you wish it, Sol," he murmurs, and I don't miss his double meaning when he flicks his eyebrows.

Before I can react his expression becomes serious. We're back in business. I forget about the view. I'm sure it's spectacular, but Lucien is far more interesting to watch.

***

In the end, Lucien finds twenty locks to fix. He's like a thing possessed as he stalks about the platforms on the tower.

The couples all blend into one, but with every resounding click, the heavy atmosphere lifts. By the time we reach the twentieth lock, there are smiles on the faces of the people on the viewing platform. Couples stand hand in hand. People hug, children laugh. Everyone seems so much happier.

It's pretty damn amazing what finding all these moments has done here. I'm still to witness a moment that is anything but ordinary, yet it feels extraordinary all the same.

"Moments are never grand or flamboyant, or even romantic sometimes," Lucien tells me as we return to our bodies, having just witnessed two people realising their love over a pot of burnt stew. I mean, how is that, in any way, a beautiful moment?

"I don't think you have a romantic bone in your body, Sol the Troll." Lucien huffs by my side.

I wink at him, and he chuckles.

"How many locks have we fixed now?" I stifle a yawn and stretch out cramped muscles. "I've lost count. They've all blended into one."

Lucien sighs heavily before replying. "I think it is forty-five, or maybe forty-six." He shrugs. "I don't know." He looks dead on his feet as he leans against the window frame. His eyes are heavy, and the dark circles beneath them are hollow. He needs to rest. We both do.

I'm so tired I don't even react to the fact we are hundreds of feet up in the air and beyond Lucien there is nothing but a pane of glass to stop him falling. Not that he would fall, obviously, since he can fly. He's a fairy.

I slump to the ground with my back to the view. It is beginning to get dark and lights have come on all over the tower. It looks pretty, but I think it's time to go. I watch Lucien as he searches for any locks we may have missed. His eyes take on a distant look, and then he shakes his head.

"There are no more locks up here. I think we can go now." He gazes at me and grins. "Can you ride the elevator back down without the need for any distraction?"

I return his smirk as he offers me a hand to help me stand. "Can you?"

I get to my feet, and he leads me back towards the lift. Before we get there, he stops and turns with a gasp. He's grinning. "There is another way." He flicks his eyebrows, and I frown.

"I ain't using the stairs, Hairy. No way. I'll go down the way we came up, thank you very much." I saw the stairs, before we got into the lift. No way will I cope walking down all those stairs with nothing to block the view except a metal cage surrounding the structure. I shudder.

"Not the stairs, Sol. I promise." He stands before me, his hands flat on my chest. "Do you trust me?"

What kind of question is that? Surely he knows I would trust him with my life, although admitting that to myself shocks me.

I place my hands gently on his hips, holding him in place, but not firmly, in case he wishes to move away. Somehow I don't think he will. I don't want him to, ever, but that is something we need to discuss later. Right now, we need to get down from this bloody tower before I fly apart at the seams.

Lucien seems buoyed by the amount of success we've had up here, and whilst I'm happy we found so many locks, I've been on edge the entire time. Being up this high has not cured me of my fear. I'm simply holding it together because I have to.

"Come on, Hairy. Let's go." I try not to sound irritable.

"Close your eyes and do not open them until I say," Lucien commands gently.

I roll my eyes instead.

"Sol!" He gives me an admonishing look. With an exaggerated sigh I do as he says. "Now, hold me tight."

"Lucien, if this is just your way of getting another kiss, you know you only have to ask."

"Do not be so bold," he rebukes. I chuckle, holding him so tight he squeaks. That's funny.

For a moment, nothing happens. I keep my eyes closed because he told me to, but I'm beginning to get a bit impatient.

"Alright then, Hairy. Whatever it is you're about to do, do it."

"It is done, mon cheri. You may open your eyes now."

With another sigh, I do so. Then I gasp. We're no longer in the tower; we're on the ground just below it. I spin around in shock.

"How the hell...?" I look at him. He's watching me with amusement twinkling in his eyes. "How did we get down?"

"C'est magique, Monsieur Troll." He clicks his fingers above his head in a flamboyant gesture and grins, before winking at me smugly.

I narrow my eyes. "You used magic to get us down when you were so tired you could barely stand straight up there?" I'm angry, and I think he's surprised that I am, but then his expression changes.

"Whether or not I use magic is not up for discussion, Sol." He folds his arms over his chest. "I'd have thought you would be grateful you did not have to ride in that elevator full of humans with their smelly feet."

"The smelly feet I could've done without, Hairy. I was looking forward to the kiss, though." I bite my lip at the admission, and he grins.

"Oh, if that is all you are angry about, then we can kiss anywhere."

"Even here?" I ask, looking around us. We are surrounded by humans, all happily oblivious to our presence.

"Even here." He presses against me, and I wrap my arms around him.

On his tiptoes, he is just tall enough to reach my lips if I bend down a little. He pulls me down, and we kiss. However, instead of the passionate embrace I was expecting, Lucien gives a soft sigh, and his tiny body goes limp in my arms. My heart stops.

"Lucien?" I hold him tight, to stop him falling. His eyes are closed and his face pale. "Hairy." I shake him urgently. There is still no response. "Lucien, bloody hell."

With a sharp intake of breath he opens his eyes. His body remains limp in my arms. His face is pale and his eyes glazed.

"Sol." His breath is shallow. "I am sorry. I…" He can't even form coherent words, he's so exhausted.

I blame myself. I should have watched him more closely. I knew he was hiding his exhaustion from me. I saw it after our kiss in the alley. We should have rested, but he was adamant that we keep going. He kept finding locks to fix. I should have been more insistent, more assertive.

This time, I won't take no for an answer.

Chapter 11: Locked in an Embrace

I SCOOP AN EXHAUSTED Lucien into my arms and hold him close to my chest.

"That's it, we're done for the day," I tell him.

"Non, mon cheri," he protests, but it's superficial. He's too tired. "We need to fix as many locks as we can today. We have to keep searching."

"Are there others still searching right now?" I ask. Lucien's eyes take on a distant look then he nods. "Right then. I'm carrying you home." He looks upset, but I'm determined not to listen to any argument from him.

"All the way?" He sounds surprised at my suggestion.

"If I have to, yes. It's really not a problem."

Lucien looks around, his expression doubtful, but I do notice he does not try to move.

"To your bridge?" He seems expectant, even a little excited by the prospect. I shake my head because why the hell would he want to go to a dark, slimy hole beneath a bridge when he has a comfortable, warm apartment?

"No, Hairy. I'm taking you to your home, where you can get some well-earned sleep on a proper bed."

He doesn't argue. I don't think he has any energy left. With a soft huff, he shuffles to get comfortable and then lays his head against my shoulder. His fingers gently glide over the front of my shirt. I fight the urge to giggle, because it tickles.

Who'd've thought I was ticklish, eh?

With him tucked against me like he was made to fit there, I carry him through the streets and alleys, trusting my instinct to follow the river, rather than remembering the way back to his apartment.

Once I find more familiar landmarks, I will be able to locate his apartment building.

Lucien feels so tiny in my arms. He's light as a feather, and as fragile and delicate. His flaming hair tickles my chin, and his unique scent fills my nostrils.

I feel I could carry him forever. I would carry him to the ends of the Earth, if he needed me to. I would protect him with my life.

The strength of this feeling is incredible. I had no idea I could feel so passionately about anything other than my bridge. I really don't know where all this passion is going to take me, though, because there's no way he can possibly feel the same about me is there? Despite the two kisses we have shared.

Too late, I remember Lucien can sense what I'm thinking, or at least what I'm feeling, when we are in physical contact. I bite my lip and look down at him.

His eyes are closed, and his breathing is deep and even. He has fallen asleep in my arms. Does that mean he feels safe? Did I do anything to make him feel that way? I've been a grumpy sod all day. He's the one who's been making all the effort. I've just been following where he led. Like he says, I may look human, but deep inside I am still a grumpy old troll. I've seen him throw up his arms in frustration on several occasions. I bet he can't wait to get rid of me after all this is done.

I don't want him to want that, though. How can I feel this way after one day in his company? It's all very confusing and new. And I'm not even sure if these emotions I'm feeling are real, or if it's because I'm locked in a human body. Will I feel the same when I return to my troll form? And if, by some miracle, Lucien does feel the same about me, will he be hurt if my feelings disappear when I'm a big ugly hairy troll? Will I be hurt if his feelings change when I change back?

Bloody hell, I need to stop overthinking this, or my head will explode.

I yawn wearily. Lucien isn't the only one who's exhausted. Except I've obviously got more stamina than him because he's already in dreamland.

That poses a bit of a problem when we eventually reach the front door of his apartment building. I can't help feeling just a little bit proud of myself for getting us here, but what now? I hate to wake him, but I have to, to get him to unlock the door.

"Lucien," I murmur into his soft auburn curls. "We're here, at your door. Wake up, sweetheart. I don't have a key."

Sweetheart? Where the hell did that come from?

"Oy, Hairy. Wake up!" That's more like it.

Lucien stirs, opens his eyes and lifts his head briefly before tucking it back into my shoulder and wrapping his arms around my neck with a soft moan.

"Touch your finger to the lock, mon cheri," he mumbles, his breath heating the fabric of my shirt as his fingers toy lightly with the hair at the back of my neck. "The door will open for you."

"Well that's not very secure." I frown, trying to juggle our position so I can do as he says without dropping him. "I mean, anyone could just walk in."

"It will only open for you or me, Sol. No one else."

"Why's that, then?" I grunt as I try to point my finger at the lock.

"Magic." He yawns and snuggles closer, if that is even possible. That's not a bloody answer, but I guess it's all I'm going to get.

He feels all soft and warm and relaxed while my body is going fucking crazy, trying to process all these sensations at once. A distraction, I need a distraction.

Getting to the lock without putting him down is proving enough to keep my mind off other stuff. I strain the last few inches and, voila! The lock is open. Fucking hell, since when did I start *thinking* in French?

Negotiating three flights of stairs without dropping him and without passing out or vomiting will provide the distraction I need. The process is not going to be fun, but necessary.

"When did you have time to cast a spell that would allow me access to your apartment, Lucien?" If I keep talking I'll be okay. "You never left my side the entire time we were in your apartment, and I know you didn't do anything when we first entered, or when we left." I'm babbling but it's working.

"The lock has always been set up to respond to your touch," Lucien murmurs.

I stop, halfway up the first flight of stairs.

"What do you mean *always*?" Does he mean since this began, this morning? Or what?

"I did it a long time ago, in the hope that... Well, I did it a long time ago," he finishes with another yawn, and I wonder if he is actually awake, or if these are just sleepy mumblings and he doesn't really know what he's saying.

I hardly think he would set his lock to respond to me before he had even met me. That's just too ridiculous, and he couldn't have predicted that he would even need to allow me access to his apartment.

I'm confused, and I don't like being confused. On a positive note, it does serve as a big enough distraction to get me the rest of the way up the stairs. That, and the fact that his apartment isn't really all that high, considering where we've just been.

Lucien's apartment door responds to my touch as well.

When we enter, I see that the shutters have been closed over the enormous panoramic window, so once I have closed the door, I can forget about how high we are. We're safe.

I look down at Lucien. His eyes are closed again. He looks content and comfortable. Maybe I should just stand here until he's had enough sleep. If I put him to bed I might disturb him, and I know how hard it is to get back to sleep when you've been disturbed.

"Are you just going to hold me here, or are you going to put me down, Sol?"

"Well, I would." I bite my lip, because I didn't mean for that to come out all snappy. "But I don't know where your bedroom is, and I didn't want to put you down on the couch in case I woke you up."

"I'm awake, so put me down."

I hesitate. He was reluctant to be carried, and if I put him down in his living room, he will find excuses not to rest. He'll want to make me something to drink, or eat, or he'll want me to look out of the window again...we can't have that.

"I think I'll just look for the bedroom, Hairy, and then there won't be anything to distract you when I do put you down."

"What do you mean, Sol?" He starts to squirm, but my hold is firm, and, at the end of the day, I am stronger than him. "Put me down," he demands.

"No! Not until I've found your bedroom."

I walk past the first door leading off his living room. I know that's the bathroom. Stepping around a laden bookshelf, I find a hidden set of stairs and groan. Why does there have to be more stairs?

"Sol. Lâchez-moi, bon sang!" Lucien struggles.

"Is your bedroom up these stairs?" I ask, ignoring his indignant tone.

"Yes, now *put me down!*"

"I'm going up the stairs. Don't struggle. You know what I'm like with heights. I can't guarantee I won't fall."

Lucien freezes with a gasp and holds onto me tightly. I didn't mean to scare him. I hope he hasn't seen that as a threat when it was actually a warning of what could happen.

"I would never let you fall, mon cheri," he whispers. His lips move against my neck, and I almost do fall, because the sensation turns my bones to liquid.

Suddenly, my heart is pounding in my ears, and my body hardens as his fingers feed through my hair at the back of my neck.

"Lucien," I almost sob, because I just can't process this at all. It's the same as when we were in that alley and in the elevator, except far more intense.

We're at the top of the stairs and in a room that overlooks Lucien's living room. I don't even remember climbing the rest of the way.

"How did we...?" I gasp. Two warm fingers press over my lips.

"Shh!" he whispers. "C'est magique, Monsieur Troll."

"Will you just stop with the using magic cra..." I stop.

I look down into eyes that are bluer than the sky. They are the sky. Why does my heart soar into the clouds when he so much as glances at me? And why am I not panicking like a gibbering wreck when it does? Trolls don't soar anywhere.

"Take me to bed, Sol," Lucien murmurs against my neck.

Yes, bed. That's why we came up here, so I could take him—I mean put him to bed. He needs to rest.

I take a deep breath to calm everything down. It's not easy, but things that were up are now on their way down again.

Lucien's bed is enormous. That fact alone is enough to pull me out of the moment.

"Bloody hell, Hairy. 'Ow big do you need your bed to be? I mean, you're fucking tiny. I bet you don't even fill a corner of this."

"Non, mon cheri." He's smiling, chuckling even. I can feel his lips moving against my skin. "But I know someone who might appreciate the size."

I look at him sharply as I reach the edge of the bed. Carefully, I lay him down on top of his covers.

"What do you mean by that?" I ask. "Who else stays here that needs such a big bed?" And why am I even thinking about that, or asking him? It's none of my bloody business who he has over.

"No one stays over, Sol—yet."

He's lying on his back, not attempting to sit. I'm still bent over him even though I'm no longer supporting his weight. It's a bit difficult to stand when his arms are wrapped around me so tightly. I try to pull away but he just pulls me back.

"Hairy!" I click my tongue. "Let go. I need to sort your bed out."

He lets go of me with a huff. His hands fall above his head, and he watches me carefully as I walk around to the other side to pull back his covers.

"Here, slide over." I tell him.

"You don't have to tuck me in, Sol." He giggles.

"I know, but it's the only way I can be sure you'll stay in bed and rest."

"I could just get up once you have gone." He regards me defiantly.

I chuckle and shake my head. "Which is why I'm going to stay to make sure you don't."

"Good." He smirks before kicking off his shoes and sliding over to tuck his feet beneath the covers.

He snuggles down, and I cover him, making sure he is comfortable and warm. His eyes are already closed and his face relaxed in sleep. He was exhausted.

I look about for somewhere to sit. I find a large, comfortable armchair. I'll sit for a few minutes to catch my breath and to make sure he really is asleep, and then I'll go back downstairs.

I'm lulled by the peace and quiet after the hectic day I've just had. I didn't intend to sleep, but my eyes are so heavy. I'll just close them for a little while.

***

I wake with a start, my neck cramped since my head has lolled against the back of the chair. I must have fallen asleep almost instantly. I was pretty tired.

I glance over at Lucien. He's still fast asleep, buried deep into his covers, his tiny body swamped in his enormous bed. Why does a tiny fairy need such a big bed anyway? It's still a puzzle.

I stand and stretch. Just one more check on Lucien's sleeping form, and then I'll go downstairs and find something to eat. I didn't realise until now, but I'm bloody starving, again.

Lucien's beauty takes my breath away. He is exquisite. His face is relaxed in peaceful slumber and his flaming hair frames his head like a fiery aura. Before I can stop myself, I have reached out to gently brush some stray strands of hair from his face.

"Lucien," I whisper, knowing he won't hear me. "What've you done to me? I don't think Madame Queen's spell was the only one cast over me last night. Except, I don't think I want to break this one."

With a sigh, I straighten up and turn away. This is a completely stupid situation. I know he's never going to want me. I'm an ugly, great troll; he's a beautiful, delicate fairy. And even if that wasn't a barrier, why would he want someone as grumpy and sullen as me?

As I reach the top of the stairs that lead down from this mezzanine floor, movement alerts me.

"Sol?" Lucien's voice sounds croaked and sleepy. "Don't go."

I sigh. He's awake, I suppose I should stay and make sure he rests more. I turn. He is sitting up in bed, watching me with wide eyes that seem to glow in the darkness.

"Come to bed, Sol." He pats the covers beside him.

There's certainly enough room for me, but feeling the way I do, I'm not sure it's such a good idea.

"I can sleep downstairs on your sofa, Hairy." I smile, grateful for his offer and wondering why I'm being a martyr, because his sofa isn't even big enough for him to sleep on.

"Sleep wasn't what I had in mind."

Breathing is suddenly a bit difficult as my brain tries to process what he's said.

"So, what did you have in mind?" I have to ask, because I can't believe he means what I think he means.

"Sol, stop thinking and come to bed," he demands, his eyes full of fire and something else I just can't allow myself to believe.

With a nervous swallow, I approach the bed and sink stiffly down onto the edge, my back to him.

"Well, I suppose I could sleep here." I shrug, trying to sound nonchalant but knowing that my voice is coming out slightly squeaky. "It's not as if there isn't room. Your bed's big enough for three trolls."

Lucien's form is suddenly draped across my back, his head pops over my shoulder, and his face draws level with mine.

"It only needs to be big enough for one troll, and a fairy." His breath is warm as he whispers low in my ear.

I can feel my entire body reacting to his touch. His fingers surf the contours of my back.

He's driving me crazy. With a sigh of surrender, I turn my head and capture his lips with mine. His sharp gasp and subsequent sigh of pleasure fires me up even more. I twist, my hands finding his shoulders and pushing as I climb further onto the bed. He falls back into the luxurious covers with a satisfied sigh. I follow, lying over him and watching, as he regards me through hooded eyes.

Those eyes that reflect the sky. I'm always all right if I can see the sky. Anything higher than me is good.

Lucien's fingers wrap around my forearms, at least as much as they can do. His expression is one of such desire I can't believe it can possibly be for me. He's going to be disappointed if he's expecting something spectacular. I think I should warn him.

"Lucien, I er, I don't get out much, you know that."

He nods, biting his lip, the action sends signals all over my body. Who knew that someone biting their own lip would do that to my body?

"What I'm tryin' to tell you, Hairy, is that—I've never done this before."

Instead of seeing disappointment in his eyes, I see the desire increase. He leaves go of my arms and his hands grasp my face, pulling me down to press my lips to his.

"Then we shall be each other's firsts." His words vibrate across my lips, and I want more of that. He tastes delicious, but his words also shock me into pulling back.

"Why—why would you want me to be your first?" I ask in complete surprise.

"Why would you want me to be yours, Sol?" Lucien's eyebrows rise, and I realise this hasn't just been one-sided.

He's been sending me signals all day, about how he regards me, how he wants more than friendship. His constant physical contact hasn't been just because he's like that with everyone. I saw that much when we were in the elevator. He withdrew, even recoiled from the touch of others, but from me, he doesn't even flinch when we touch. He actively seeks the contact.

"I want you so much, Sol. Make love to me, please."

"Oh my god," I exclaim as he pulls me down with a chuckle.

He's still laughing as our lips touch. I pull back again, still unable to believe this is happening.

"Lucien." I want to be absolutely certain before this goes too far. "Are you sure this is what you want? I mean me? You haven't forgotten this isn't really what I look like, have you?"

"And have you forgotten that I do not usually look like this?" Lucien smiles. "It's because we are in human form that we can do this, Sol, and I have not forgotten what you really look like. It's because of what you are, and who you are, that I am absolutely, without any doubt, certain this is what I want."

For a moment, his confession takes my breath away. As he watches me patiently I put aside any lingering doubt and dive in.

Our lips crush together, and he gasps, then moans, opening to me. His tongue darts out to find mine. He tastes amazing and the feel of his tongue brushing against mine sends shocks throughout my body. Those same shocks of sensation I have been feeling since we first met. It had nothing to do with the transformation, or the body I am locked inside, and everything to do with him.

Lucien's legs fall apart as we kiss, and I crowd between them. I know he said this was only possible because we are in human form, but he is still so small compared to me. How is this going to work? I wasn't lying when I said I'd never done this before. I haven't, and neither has he. It's the blind leading the blind here.

"Stop overthinking, Sol. Do what you feel," Lucien murmurs as he pulls me down. "I'm yours and you are mine. We will not hurt each other, we cannot."

He sits up, and I kneel, sitting back on my heels. Lucien pulls his shirt over his head and throws it across the room. His hands tug at the hem of mine, and I lift my arms to allow it to be pulled off too.

He shuffles forwards and straddles my lap. He gives a groan of satisfaction as his hands spread across my chest. His fingers play through the hair there. I can't help giggling. His caress tickles.

"You are the one we should call hairy." Lucien smiles, his eyes wide. "I had no idea you would be ticklish." He laughs as I squirm at his touch again.

Our lips crash together, and his tongue searches for mine. I am lost to this sensation, lost to him as he makes me completely his.

My hands ache to touch him everywhere. My thumbs caress his ribs. He gasps and tips his head back in ecstasy. His hair falls in luscious waves down his back, and my breath catches in my throat.

He lifts his head back to face me.

"You take my breath away, Sol," he murmurs, kissing a line along my jaw to my ear.

"You're the one that's beautiful, Lucien. Bloody hell." He clamps his lips down onto my neck, and the sensation goes straight to my already straining groin.

Suddenly clothes are too much. I was just getting used to wearing them as well. Now I just want rid of them. I want to feel as much of my skin touching Lucien's as possible.

I wrap my arms around him and tip him onto his back. The swiftness of the move takes him by surprise, and he cries out, but I don't let him fall. I lower him the last few inches slowly.

"I would never let you fall either, Lucien," I whisper to him, my lips against his neck. "I need you naked now. I need us both naked."

"Let me help you with that request." He grins. He lifts his hand and clicks his fingers.

The rest of our clothes disappear, and Lucien raises his eyebrows wickedly then lifts his hips to meet mine.

I am lost to him. Whatever we do now, we do together. We are together.

I feed my hand between us and take hold of his slender length. With a gasp, he closes his eyes. I think he is lost, too, in the sensation of my hand touching him.

"Oui, Sol. Juste comme ça. Touchez-moi là-bas."

I feel a certain satisfaction that I have managed to make him babble incoherently in French, but I don't really know what I'm doing. Instinct takes over as his tiny hand grasps my hardened cock. Thought escapes me, and I gasp. With our hands around each other's shafts, I lean in and capture his lips.

"Bon…mon cheri. Oui…bien," he gasps as we move as one.

We've never done this, but we find our rhythm so swiftly, as if we are each in tune with the other's needs and desires. We have spent all day inside each other's thoughts. I guess it's inevitable, and watching so many couples experience the first time they realised their love for each other has our own emotions in a turmoil.

"Sol!" Lucien cries out as his body trembles. He opens his eyes, and his free hand grasps my shoulder convulsively.

His cock throbs in my hand, and my fingers are coated in warm, sticky liquid. The sound he makes, and the smell of his release, tips me over the edge. I come with a grunt, my own release so intense I see stars.

I collapse in a boneless heap, and my beautiful fairy falls beside me.

For a moment, I just lie there, breathless and spent.

"Bloody hell, Hairy," I gasp. "That was a bit extreme for a goodnight kiss."

Lucien snorts and shuffles so he is tucked into my side. I wrap my arm about him and pull him close. We should be sticky right now, but I think, by another act of magic, Lucien has taken care of it.

"I wish you would stop using magic and rest, you bloody minx." I huff. My eyes are growing heavy, and I can feel my body succumbing to sleep.

"I will rest now, mon amour." He snuggles even closer, and I feel him relax.

I think he's fallen asleep until he speaks again.

"Sol?"

"You should be asleep," I tell him firmly. He snuggles in, his hand caressing lazily over my chest.

"I will sleep, I promise, but you must promise me something, too."

"What?"

"Stay with me."

"I ain't goin' anywhere." I chuckle. "Besides, your couch is far too small for me to sleep on. This bed's massive."

He snorts. "That is not what I meant."

He smiles at me as I turn to face him, propping my head on my hand.

"What did you mean, then?"

"I meant don't go back to your bridge when this is all over. Stay with me here."

I think my heart might have just skipped several beats.

"For how long?" I ask in complete shock. "I mean, what the hell, Hairy? I'll be back to being a troll after all this is over. I won't even fit in your front door."

"You don't always have to be a troll, Sol. You can be like me. Take human form when you wish it."

"And then what? What would we be?"

"We would be together."

He makes it all sound so simple, and maybe it is. Maybe that's all it needs to be: a case of simply wanting something. And I want, so much. I never knew I could want anything as much as I want this.

"I think I'd like that, Hairy." I kiss the top of his head where it is tucked into the crook of my shoulder. Then my eyes close, and we finally give in to sleep.

Chapter 12: Locked in a Dilemma

W HEN I WAKE, it is still dark. At first, I don't understand what has woken me. Lucien is still tucked neatly into my side like he belongs there. I don't think he's moved even a millimetre.

For a moment, I listen to his steady, even breaths and simply enjoy the feel of his body lying next to mine.

Then the reason I woke becomes clear. I need to empty my bladder, like right now. Damn this human body. As a troll I can go for centuries without needing to piss. As a human I can't go more than a few hours.

With a certain urgency, I move, careful not to disturb the sleeping beauty by my side. He stirs but doesn't wake, settling into the warm space I have left, with a small, contented smile on his face. A shock of attraction shoots through me. He's beautiful, my little fairy. I lean in and softly kiss his cheek.

Lucien's bathroom is downstairs. The need to go overrules my anxiety about the height.

I negotiate the stairs and then the intricacies of a human bathroom with more ease than I really thought I could.

Feeling rather smug with myself, I walk through the door into Lucien's living room and come face-to-face with Madame Queen.

"What the fu…? What are you doing here?" I hiss.

"I could ask the same of you, Monsieur Troll." She raises her eyebrows as she casually examines her fingernails.

She's dressed a little less formally than she was the first time we met. She looks none the less regal, though, in a long, silvery, off-the-shoulder dress that flows to the floor and across it in waves of material and glitter.

"What I'm doin' 'ere is none of your business, Queenie." I glance up at Lucien's mezzanine bedroom and keep my voice down as low as possible so as not to disturb him.

"Do not worry about Lucien. He will not hear you."

I gasp. "What've you done to 'im? If you've hurt 'im…" I take a step towards her, and she looks almost joyful that I am even attempting to intimidate her. With a flick of her wrist, I am frozen in place.

"Such fierceness, troll." She chuckles. "Tell me, what would you do if I had hurt him?"

I feel my heart skip a beat at the thought, but anger wells up from within me, so fierce, I feel I could actually take on the queen of all the fairy folk. I struggle against the restraint she has placed on me.

Tears of frustration and panic form in my eyes as I fight to free myself.

~Lucien!

"Oh, do not worry yourself, troll. He is safe." Madame Queen sounds completely unaffected by my fear. "I would never harm one of my own." She flicks her wrist again, and I fall to my knees as the restraint is lifted.

"What do you want?" I growl at her.

"I want to restore you to your former body, troll." She smiles down at me as if she is bestowing a reward. I sense an ulterior motive though.

"Why?" I ask, pulling myself to my feet and forgetting that I'm naked.

She regards me with wide eyes and then clicks her fingers. I am suddenly clothed, but not in the comfortable clothing that Lucien chose for me. She's put me in some sort of suit, with a tie around my neck. I feel like I'm being strangled. With a grunt, I undo it and throw it across the room.

"Tell me why you're here?" I growl, louder this time, because she is trying my patience.

"I told you." She smiles, annoyingly calm and condescending. "I wish to—"

"The real reason." I scowl, folding my arms across my chest, and tap my foot. "You said one hundred locks. Lucien and I have only fixed forty-six. I can't imagine you're the type of person who would relent on the final fifty-four, so stop beatin' about the bloody bush and tell me the truth."

Madame Queen regards me angrily. Her auburn hair flies about her head like a halo and she rises up into the air, puffing out her chest. A fiery aura surrounds her, and despite her size, she is quite fearsome and intimidating. Then, to my surprise, she seems to deflate. With a heavy sigh, she sits on Lucien's sofa and gestures for me to join her.

"Please sit, Sol. I wish to talk to you."

I don't want to sit and have a cosy chat with her. I want to be back in bed with Lucien, holding him against me, listening to his steady breaths and fluttering heartbeat. It might be the last chance I get.

The queen's expression intrigues me, though. I get the feeling she is very anxious about something.

I sit.

For a moment, Madame Queen remains silent, clasping her hands nervously in her lap and staring out at the night sky, visible through Lucien's enormous window. I chance a look, no longer feeling as afraid of the height, and gasp. It is quite beautiful, even if it is tinted orange by the city lights.

It isn't as beautiful as Lucien, though. Nothing could ever compare to him.

"You cannot stay with him, Sol." The queen's tone is sad. She continues to stare out at the night.

"What do you mean, I can't stay?" I turn to glare at her. "No one gets to decide that but Lucien and me. It's none o' your business. You don't get a say."

"On the contrary." Madame Queen turns to face me. Her expression is pure steel, but I still see a hint of the sadness from before. "I do have a say. I am the queen, and I will protect my own—protect Lucien."

I make a face, curling my lip at her statement. "Protect 'im from what?"

"From you."

I gasp. "But that's ridiculous. I'd never hurt 'im." I give her a fierce scowl. "I'd never let anyone else hurt 'im either."

Madame Queen nods, and for the first time relaxes a little. "I was hoping you would say that."

I get the feeling I'm not going to like whatever she's about to say.

"I know you would never hurt him intentionally. Nevertheless, you are hurting him by simply being here."

"How?" I feel faint. How can I be hurting him? Everything we did tonight was amazing. He would have stopped me if I was hurting him. I'm beginning to panic. I take a deep breath to calm down.

"Lucien is sick, Sol."

"What?" My heart's going to stop beating altogether if she springs any more news like that on me. Except it isn't news. I knew, or I suspected already. She's just confirmed it. "How sick?"

"Very sick. He almost died."

I scoff at her statement, because it's too ludicrous. "Fairies are immortal. They don't die."

"Oh, Sol." When Madame Queen turns to look at me, she has tears in her eyes. "If only that were true."

I swallow hard against a lump of emotion the size of a boulder in my throat.

"You ain't kiddin', are ya?" I hold my breath, willing her to say this whole thing is a joke. She shakes her head.

"No, Sol. I wish I was."

"What's wrong with 'im?" I don't think I want to know the answer. I have this urge to run upstairs, gather Lucien in my arms and shut out the world. Perhaps if I do that, this thing that's making him sick will go away. "He can't be sick." I gasp. "He can't. He just can't. Tell me what's wrong with him, please?" I wipe at tears that just won't stop. "I'll do anything to help him. Anything."

"Are you sure, Sol? Anything?" Madame Queen regards me with steely fervour. She's going to hold me to that offer.

"I didn't just say it for the good of my health." I gasp again, a sobbing breath. Trolls don't cry. I didn't even know it was physically possible. But even a creature with a stone for a heart couldn't help but be reduced to tears when faced with news like this. "Oh, God! I could lose him. I can't lose him. He's too precious."

"He is precious to us all." Madame Queen seems moved to tears as well. I didn't think she had it in her. She's as emotional as the rest of us. Who knew?

For a moment, I can't speak. I can't form the words that I need to say. My throat has closed up, and I can't even swallow. Eventually, I manage to find a suitable gap between the sniffs and the sobs. I think two thousand years' worth of tears have fallen in the last two minutes.

"Just tell me what I need to do," I whisper hoarsely.

"You must leave." Madame Queen holds my gaze, unblinking. "You must leave and never come back."

"What?" I sniff, wiping my nose on the back of my sleeve. She's gone barking mad. "Why the hell would I leave? Haven't you heard what I've just said?"

"I heard, and you told me you would do anything."

"Anything but that."

"Even if your presence here is what is making Lucien sick?"

My heart stops completely. "How can I be the cause of Lucien's illness? We only just met properly yesterday, and you said he'd been sick for a long time."

"Three hundred years, to be exact."

Three hundred years. Why does that sound familiar? Three hundred years. I repeat the number in my head until it dawns on me.

"That's how long Lucien said he'd stood watch over my bridge."

"Yes, that's right. His illness began then." The queen looks away, as if there is something she wants to hide from me.

"Oh my god. Is it me? Am I making him sick? How, though? This can't be happening. This is a nightmare."

"Sol." Madame Queen takes my hands in hers, and I'm shocked, until I realise that she's done it to stop mine from trembling. "I am going to ask you something very important and very intimate, and I am sorry, but I must, because you need to hear the answer, too." I sniff and nod, giving her permission. "Do you love Lucien?"

If my breathing gets any shallower I am going to pass out. Do I love Lucien? I don't even have to think about the answer to her question.

"Yes!" I growl, because I feel this with more passion and more certainty than I have ever felt in my entire troll life. "Yes," I say again, just to emphasise the tiny word that seems so inadequate in a situation like this.

"If you truly love him, Sol, you must let him go."

I'm feeling petulant and stubborn now. Why must I let go of the one good thing that has ever happened to me in two thousand years.

"What if I don't want to let him go?" I lift my chin in defiance.

"Then he will die."

And there it is, the one and only reason that could ever persuade me to leave. I don't even question her, because I can see in her eyes she is telling me the truth.

"But I've only just found him." My voice is no more than a hoarse whisper. "I didn't even know I was looking."

I didn't even know how much I needed him. How can this be happening?

"I know." Madame Queen nods her head, dabbing at her eyes delicately. "And I'm sorry, Sol. I'm so sorry. But it is the only way. Trolls and fairies, they cannot be together. He has stood watch over your bridge for three centuries and would not listen to any of us when we warned him what could happen. We watched him fade, and grow weak. He has pined for you, when all this time his love has been in vain."

"But it ain't in vain. I love him back." I'm clutching at straws now, because I know full well my love is never going to be good enough. Lucien deserves so much better.

"That love cannot last. It's just not possible. If you stay, you will both be miserable and it will only end in tragedy."

I bloody knew this couldn't last. I knew it was a pipe dream. All those things Lucien said to me. We let ourselves believe all those whispered dreams we shared in the dark. But in the end they've just disappeared in a puff of smoke.

With a heavy, shuddering sigh, I resign myself to a life alone. I was happy with that life before I met Lucien. Why shouldn't I be happy again? I just need to find the positives. I just need time. A lot of time.

"Where do I go, then?" I don't look up. "Back to my bridge?"

"Non. Your bridge is too close. If you go back there, Lucien will just go back to standing watch, waiting for you to appear. He must think you have gone, and gone for good. You must leave the city."

"But I don't know anywhere." I don't even feel despair at this news. I don't feel anything. I'm numb. "I know this was what you wanted. To move me on. Lucien told me he persuaded you to leave me where I was."

"Against my better judgement." Madame Queen nods. "Do not worry, Sol. We will not leave you homeless. I know a place you can go. A peaceful place. Where there are very few people to disturb you. There is no danger of a city being built around you while you hibernate, and there is even a bridge for you to live beneath if you wish."

"Sounds great," I whisper. My strength has left me. I can't even thank her.

It's all I ever wanted. All I could have hoped for, but it's nothing without him. If I can't share it with Lucien, it will all be empty and soulless. I'll go there, curl up beneath that bridge and sleep. With any luck, I might not ever wake up.

"You must promise never to come back here, Sol," Madame Queen continues gently. "You must promise never to seek Lucien out, for his sake."

"I promise," I answer mechanically. I promised him I'd stay. What's he going to think when he wakes and I've gone? But I can't keep my promise to him if it ends up killing him, can I?

The queen nods in satisfaction. She stands as if getting ready to do something important.

"I will return you to your troll form whenever you are ready."

I look up, startled. I'd completely forgotten about that. This is what I was working towards, what Lucien was working so tirelessly to help me achieve. I knew he was exhausting himself. I should've stopped him, but I didn't. It's just another reminder of how very selfish I am. I could never have made him happy. Not in a million years.

I can't stand the pity in Madame Queen's eyes as she waits for my answer, or the guilt, or the pain or anything. If she wants to change me back, she can. I don't give a shit what I look like or what form I'm stuck in. Nothing matters anymore.

"When do you want me to leave?" My voice doesn't even sound real to me now. Nothing does.

"Now."

"Without even saying goodbye to him?"

"It is better this way. If he thinks you have left without a word, he will recover more quickly."

"But he'll think I abandoned him." I think of how he will react when he wakes to find me gone. Will he be upset? Will he try to find me anyway? "At least let me leave a note."

"No!" Madame Queen snaps. She sounds impatient now. "Leaving without a word is the only way to ensure he will not try to find you. He will be angry, but that will help him get over you. It will help him heal."

But what about me? How will I heal? How am I ever going to recover from this? I want to ask her, but somehow I don't think she is interested in my health. She wants only what is best for Lucien.

I suppose that's only right. He deserves the best. He doesn't deserve a grumpy old sod of a troll whose very presence has made him ill.

"How long do I have?"

"I have everything ready for you to leave down at your old bridge, Sol."

I nod. "There's some stuff I need to pick up from my house."

"Very well. I will accompany you there."

"And I want to say goodbye to Lucien," I add quickly.

"Non, you promised." Madame Queen looks suddenly furious, but also full of panic.

"Don't worry, I don't want to wake him up. Whatever you did to put him to sleep, you can keep doing it. But I'm never gonna see him again, at least let me set eyes on him one more time before I leave forever."

She relents. "Do not touch him. I will wait for you at your bridge. You have ten minutes, Sol."

I nod, standing stiffly. My muscles have seized after all the forced activity today. Trolls just aren't built for any kind of exercise. They're not built for walking around, holding hands, kissing, making love. Just as well I have to leave, really. It'd do me in, all that sex. But by God, I'd die a happy troll.

I climb the stairs back to Lucien's bedroom as Madame Queen disappears from the room, leaving a sprinkling of glitter everywhere.

Lucien is sleeping where I left him. I was surprised when he didn't wake before, but of course, now I know why. Madame Queen has him held in a spell. He looks peaceful and blissfully oblivious to the turmoil surrounding him.

I sit on the edge of the bed. *Don't touch him*, she said, but how can I not? I reach across and brush a lock of his beautiful hair out of his face. His skin is pale in the moonlight. It glows. It is almost moonlight itself, as delicate and precious.

"You're precious to me, Hairy," I whisper. "That's what I told her. She said you were precious to everyone, but not as much as you are to me. You're special and it could've been beautiful. It was beautiful, but it's not to be. I can't let you waste away to nothing because I want you to be mine. That's more selfish than the act of opening all those love locks just because I wanted a good night's sleep."

I sigh and hang my head. Unconsciously my fingers have begun to stroke his cheek.

"I'll always be yours, Lucien. That'll never change. I know you can never ever know that, and I'm sorry. I have to go without properly saying goodbye, so this will have to do. This will have to last me an eternity."

I lean in and kiss his soft, warm cheek. I take a deep breath, breathing in his scent for the last time.

"Bye, Hairy. Get better and have an amazing life." I sob, tears dripping down my cheeks to form small circles of wet despair on his bed sheets. "I love you."

And then I walk away from the only chance I ever had at true happiness.

A pain shoots through my heart as it breaks in two.

Chapter 13: Locked in the Moment

B ACK ON MY bridge, standing there for the last time, Madame Queen hands me a map as I sling my sack of meagre belongings on my back.

As promised, she has returned me to troll form.

"The change is permanent, Sol. You will no longer have to spend any time as a human."

"Good. I hated bein' that—bald," I grumble. If I remember how grumpy I've always been as a troll, I can block out all the other emotions that are threatening to reduce me to a quivering wreck at her feet.

"This map will show you where your new home is located," she explains. "Remember your promise, Sol. You cannot ever return."

"Madame?" I look down at her with a frown, because I can't leave without checking a couple of things. "About all the locks."

"The last ones are being fixed as we speak," she assures me. "You would not have found enough tomorrow anyway."

"So you would've let me go through all of that, even though you knew I would never have been able to finish the task?"

She shrugs. "I could not have ever predicted you would become so attached to my...to Lucien, so quickly. Although I did hope he would have charmed you enough by the second day so that I could make my offer anyway."

"You knew he felt this way about me?"

"Oui." She shrugs again. "And I knew you would feel this way about him. I am the queen, after all. This is my job. I am just sorry it could never be for the two of you."

I heave a deep sigh, stare out over the river and then down at my bridge one last time.

"He'll be all right, won't he?"

She's already assured me that my leaving will keep him from harm. I need to hear it one last time.

"I will make sure that he is, Sol." She smiles sadly. "He will recover and live a very long life. I promise you that."

I nod. "Good." I give her a weak, half smile. "Well, good riddance to bad rubbish, I'm sure you're sayin'. I'm off."

I never was one for goodbyes. It's easier not to dwell. It saves a lot of tears.

I turn and walk away. At the end of the bridge, I turn back. Madame Queen has gone. The streetlights flicker and reflect off a sprinkling of glitter on the ground, the only indication she'd been there at all.

I start to walk again, leaving behind the only life I've ever known and the only chance I ever had of being happy.

***

On the outskirts of the city, on the top of a hill overlooking the sprawling metropolis below, it begins to rain. Steady, fat, wet drops. I feel my fur beginning to soak. Great, just what I need, wet fur. I'll stink for days until it dries out.

My feet are aching like crazy. It feels like I've been walking forever. I got used to wearing shoes, and now, my bare troll feet are sore. I think I must be going soft.

I could have asked to be sent via magic to my new destination. I'm sure Madame Queen would have obliged. She couldn't get rid of me fast enough. I wanted to walk, though, to see this city that's been my home for two thousand years. This city that's grown around me, that I didn't even know anything about until yesterday.

I complained about how grey and how noisy and smelly it was, but the truth is, it's the only home I've ever known. And now, some of my fondest memories are held within its streets.

I turn and take one last look at the city spread out behind me. I can't really say I'm attached to the place itself, since I never ventured further than my bridge. But it isn't Paris I'll miss; it's the person that showed me this city for the first time.

Now I have a new home to go to. A new bridge to live underneath. A new life to forge. I should be happy about that, at least. It's what I wanted: somewhere I won't be disturbed, where I can live my life in peace. So why do my feet feel like lead weights, heavier with every step I take away from Paris?

I made the right decision. For Lucien's sake, I promised I would leave and never come back. I can't keep stopping and looking behind. What am I expecting? Lucien to come running after me? I know he can't. Even if he wants to, I'm pretty sure that queen of his will keep him asleep until I'm well gone. I very much doubt that telling Lucien where I've gone will be high on her list of priorities, either.

She won't even tell him it was her idea, because she wants him to think I've abandoned him.

"Lucien will be better off without me, for certain."

"And who exactly gets to make that decision?"

I whirl around to see Lucien standing in the middle of the lane. It's Lucien, but as I've never seen him before. He's in fairy form, and he's stunning.

His arms are folded across his naked chest, and his eyes are narrowed to dark, glowing slits. His hair flies about his head like tongues of flame, sparkling like it's charged with static. His gossamer wings are unfurled behind him, shining like shimmering gold lace. His skin has an incredible, other-worldly golden glow. He is beautiful and very angry.

"You left without saying goodbye." His eyes flash dangerously.

"Lucien, what the hell? You can't be here." I feel panic rising within me. He's putting himself in danger just being near me. He has to leave.

Lucien narrows his eyes, his hands thrust angrily on his hips as he hovers a few inches from the ground. I'm fascinated. I've always wanted to see him fly. I snap out of it. What is he doing here?

"How did you even find me?"

"I waited for you for three hundred years," he hisses. "I watched over you and your bridge. Do you not think I would have learned to sense where you were and what you were doing at all times?"

"But you were asleep when I left. She put you under a spell." I gasp at the same time he does—me because I've given the game away, and him because I think he knows who I mean.

"Madame Queen asked you to leave without saying goodbye?" He gently lowers to the ground, his face creased in a frown. "Why? And why would you just go like that? Without a fight?"

I look down at him. He's the tiniest, most exquisite thing I've ever seen, but he shouldn't be here. How can I get him to leave?

"I ain't hangin' around to answer all your stupid questions, Hairy. I've got places to go, and things to do. Now why don't you just bugger off and leave me alone?"

"Sol!" He gasps, lifting up on his wings again.

Before my eyes, he changes. He's no longer a fairy, he's now the Lucien I recognise: Lucien in human form. He moves towards me, but I pull myself to my full, impressive troll height. I have to be strong.

"Didn't you 'ear what I said?" I shout at him in desperation. He does look intimidated. That's good. Maybe I can scare him off. He'd hate me even more if I did that. "You have to go back where you belong."

"But I belong here with you, Sol. You belong with me." He pleads, his hand reaching out to touch me. "You promised."

"It was a pipe dream, Hairy." I step back, because I know I'll lose my resolve if he touches me. "I was affected by all those human emotions and, stuck in that human body, I let them take over." I hope he can't see that I'm lying through my teeth. "I'm back to being a troll now, and my heart's made of stone, not fluff."

"Don't lie to me." He sobs. "You don't believe that, I can see it in your eyes."

I put my hands over my ears because I don't want to hear it. I can't listen to his despair. I turn from him so he can't see my eyes. He doesn't know the whole truth. I can't let him see it. He has to hate me. It's the only way.

"Lucien, just go." I start to walk away. I have to.

"Sol!"

"Leave me alone!" I yell at him. Why won't he listen? Why won't he just go? "You can't...I can't..."

Suddenly I'm in his arms, and I don't know how.

"Sol, please tell me what's wrong." He sobs, his tears soaking my fur as he holds me where we've collapsed on the ground. "Tell me why you left. What could she have possibly said to you to make you break your promise to me?"

I've never felt such anguish. But because all the good is undone and there's nothing left to lose, I tell him everything Madame Queen told me. Then perhaps he will understand and leave.

"But that's ridiculous," Lucien spits, standing and pacing in front of me, muttering in French.

I stand too, hoping this means he'll be leaving. I hope he realises that I'm just a selfish old bastard for wanting to be with him when it could cause him such harm.

"I promised your queen I'd leave and never come back. She said it was the only way to be sure you recovered," I explain to him. "I promised I would never seek you out."

"But I did not make that same promise, Sol," he growls. Swifter than I have ever seen him move, he is suddenly directly in front of me. Our eyes are level, and I realise his feet are not touching the ground. He's flying again. "I was not even given the choice."

"I-If you did have the choice...?" I leave the question hanging. I know he doesn't have any choice. Neither of us do, because if I did, I would not have left him, and we would still be lying in his bed, in each other's arms right now, instead of standing in the middle of this dark, lonely lane.

His beauty has me dumbstruck, and I want him, more than I have ever wanted anything, but why does he want me? Looking like this? He's a fairy, I'm a troll. He's so incredibly beautiful, and I'm so incredibly ugly. How is this ever going to work?

"You know I have never thought you ugly, Sol." Lucien's expression softens as he reaches out to touch my cheek.

I lean into the touch with a moan. His fingers play through the fur on my face. I close my eyes and savour the moment I am sure will be the last I ever have with him. I'm certain he only means to say goodbye. If only—

"Open your eyes, Sol, please." I do. Even in his human form, he is glowing, but then he always did. "Look down at yourself."

I gasp. I never felt a thing, but I am human again, just like him.

"How the bloody hell...?"

"You wished it." Lucien smiles, watching me, searching my face as his fingertips continue their play across my cheek. "We cannot mate as fairy and troll. Madame Queen told you the truth. But in our human forms, we can set the world on fire, or the sheets, whichever pleases you best. She did not tell you that you can change between forms as easily as I do?"

"No she didn't." I'm feeling a bit cross about that. "She lied to me. Why?"

"She did not lie, Sol. She only told you half the truth, to protect me." Lucien sighs and looks away sadly. "She did tell you the truth when she said I had been sick."

"Then you shouldn't be here, should you?" I'm cross with him now, for not doing as he's told. "I need you safe and well, Hairy, not risking your life chasin' after me."

"I would not be risking my life, Sol. The life you are going to lead now will be far better for me than the life I would lead alone in the city."

I bite my lip. "Then why would your queen be so adamant that the only way was for me to leave you behind?"

"She is a queen, and she loves all of her subjects." Lucien defends her as he always has. I would expect nothing less from him. He is loyal to a fault. "She wishes to protect everyone as best she can. That protective streak becomes a little screwed when it comes to family. My sister can be too overprotective sometimes."

"Wait?" I gape. "Your what?"

Lucien grins, stroking my cheek and closing the gap so we are pressed together. My hands automatically grasp his hips to keep him in place.

"My sister, Sol. Madame Queen is my sister."

I roll my eyes and shake my head. "Well that explains everything, doesn't it?"

It doesn't quite explain everything, but it explains the exchanges I witnessed between Lucien and Madame Queen when this all began. It explains Madame Queen's need to get rid of me as fast as she could, because she knew I might eventually discover holes in her argument. It explains a lot of the things Lucien has said over the last three days. His being given the partner he wanted. The fact that he was allowed to watch over my bridge for three hundred years without being given any other assignments. He can do what he wants, he's bloody royalty.

"You could've told me." I scowl. "Instead of leaving me in the dark like that."

"What good would knowing have done?" Lucien tips his head to one side. "She would merely have played upon your knowledge to manipulate you into making the same decision."

I suppose he's right, and it makes no difference to me who he is, or who he's related to. The fact remains that he shouldn't be here. I cup his face in my hands, stroking my thumbs across his bottom lip. My skin tingles as always at the contact. I might as well make the most of it, while I can. This could still be my last chance.

"You still need to go back, Lucien," I urge gently. "Your sister, she's done all this for a reason. She wouldn't've been so manipulative if there wasn't a need to protect you." She manipulated me, sure, but for his sake. She played on my need to protect him.

"I do not need her protection, Sol, or yours." He brushes my hands away and holds an angry finger beneath my nose. "And I am perfectly capable of deciding my own fate, thank you very much."

"What if being with me really does make you sick?" How can I make him see this is not a good idea? For his sake, he needs to go back home. I can't be responsible for his death.

"Oh, Sol. My beautiful, noble, handsome troll." Lucien grabs my face, pulling me down to touch his forehead to mine. The move is so tender, so intense, I catch my breath. "Being without you was what was making me sick in the first place."

Eh? I pull back to frown at him.

"Okay, you're gonna have to explain that one to me, because just... What?"

"Sol, three centuries ago, I dreamt that you and I would be together." He has a mad fervour in his eyes as I gape at him. Now I'm beginning to think the sickness might be in his head.

"You had a premonition? About us?"

"Oui! And I did not tell anyone, because, well, I am a fairy and you are a troll."

"Right! Finally he gets it." I throw my hands up, but he catches them, draws them down and wraps them back around his waist.

"I tried to find out as much as I could about you, but no one knew anything. Your presence beneath the bridge predated Fée records."

"By about a thousand years, I reckon."

Lucien nods. "So, the only way to get to know anything about you was to sit in permanent watch over your bridge." He hangs his head. "Unfortunately, everyone saw that as a sign I was not quite well."

"Obviously." I snort. "Because why would anyone choose to do that? It must have been the most tedious three hundred years of your fairy life."

He grins. "Everyone thought so except me. But they did not know I was pining for you. It sapped my energy. Everyone thought that it was your fault."

"But how could you pine for me? We hadn't even met."

"I know, and that was what made it all seem even crazier. No one had seen hide nor hair of you for centuries. No one even knew if you were still there."

"You could've just knocked on my door." I shrug. "It seems like a simple solution. Why didn't anyone ever think of it?"

"Everyone was afraid of your reaction."

"Alright, I know I've got a bit of a rep, but come on. They were goats, and those hooves, bloody hell. They drove me bloody mad for weeks. That argument just got a bit out of hand that's all, and the goat gave me what for anyway. I don't know why everyone was so afraid of me. Wait?" I gasp. "Were you afraid of me?"

"Non, mon cheri." He cups my face in his hands. "I knew you would never hurt me, but there were rules to obey. I broke them when I spoke to you that night. But I had seen you so very rarely that I was determined to pluck up the courage to approach you the next time you emerged."

"So you did, and then I went and messed it all up by casting that spell."

"You did not mess it up, Sol. I did." Lucien hangs his head again, like he's going to make another confession. "It is my fault that humans began leaving locks on your bridge. I did not realise it, but my pining for you was so great it could be sensed even by humans. The magic aura it created was enough for humans to choose your bridge, out of all the bridges in Paris, to be the one where they felt safest to lock their love. If we'd only realised that, then all of this could have been avoided. But I never told anyone what it was that was making me so sick."

"And then you met me, and it turned the world on its head." I'm finding all of this very hard to believe, but there is a glimmer of hope in my addled, exhausted brain. "So it's not being with me that's bad for you, it's being without me?"

"Oui, mon cheri!" Lucien smiles warmly as his arms snake around my waist.

"So I left for nothing then?" All that anguish and pain, and tears were all because a sister was protecting her brother.

"Not for nothing. Your leaving proved you were willing to do anything to keep me safe." Lucien smiles. "Not even my stubborn, overprotective sister can argue with that."

"I suppose not." I shrug. "I did it because I love you, Hairy. You know that, right?" I grin at his gasp of surprise. "Did you doubt it, even for a second?"

He returns my grin. "I never doubted, mon amour. I love you, Sol the Troll." He giggles as I growl and pull him close.

Suddenly we're kissing like there's no tomorrow.

His tongue is tracing a line along my bottom lip, and I'm just beginning to wonder whether that hedge lining the road would be a comfortable place to spend the rest of the night when I feel something hard, cold and metal at the back of my neck. I pull back to find Lucien is holding an open padlock.

"What the 'ell are you doin' with that?" As if we haven't seen enough of those over the last twenty-four hours.

He's grinning wickedly as he twirls the lock on his finger. He gives me a hooded, coy look.

"This is our lock, Sol. If you will have me as your mate."

"Seriously? I mean, I know we've just declared our love for each other, but why would you want it sealed in a lock forever more?"

"Because we belong together, Sol." He says this like it should be understood, like he should never even have to explain it.

"And why would you want to belong to a grumpy, hairy old sod like me?"

"Because I happen to love this grumpy, hairy old sod." Lucien snorts. "Sol." He smiles, and it's dazzling. He takes my breath away, he really does. "Don't you see what this is?"

"No! Why don't you tell me?" I grin like a mad man. I can't help it. Just the thought of being with him forever is making me deliriously happy. I don't need it sealed up in a padlock. It's never going to fade, this feeling, this love I feel for him.

Lucien leans close, pulling me down so he can whisper in my ear.

"This is our moment."

I gasp. My heart skips a beat. We're standing in a deserted country lane on top of a hill overlooking the most romantic city in the world, as the sun begins to rise behind us. The dawn chorus is in full swing as the stars in the sky give way to the day.

"Well, all right then." I nod. "This is more like it. Forgive me for not recognising it, but all the others were so boring, I never knew ours would be so incredible."

"Urgh! Trolls," Lucien groans, but he's smiling as I pull him closer. "So what do you say?" He waves the lock in front of my face.

"We don't have a bridge to lock it to." I huff.

"Aren't we travelling to a bridge right now? What does it say on your map?"

I forgot about the map. I do have a bridge. My new bridge, that Madame Queen has given to me. I frown.

"But what if some grumpy old troll undoes this one because he wakes up in a bad mood one day?"

"I know that he would never do that to this lock." Lucien traces a finger down my cheek. "Besides, once this lock is sealed, nothing can undo it."

"And how is that, then, Hairy?"

"C'est magique, Monsieur Troll."

The End (Or perhaps it's the beginning)

About Dawn Sister

Dawn is from the North East of England. Her life is spent juggling. The juggling balls are: children, husband, work (occasionally), voluntary work, professional knitting (notice she doesn't class this as work), and writing. When she has time she actually sleeps.

The whole point of writing for Dawn is just to get it all off her chest and out of her head. If she doesn't write it down then she ends up having long conversations with the characters out loud and her husband thinks she's crazy.

Contact & Media

Twitter: www.twitter.com/dawnsister1

Tumblr: dawnsister.tumblr.com

Facebook: www.facebook.com/DawnSister

Goodreads: www.goodreads.com/DawnSister

Beaten Track: www.beatentrackpublishing.com/dawnsister

By Dawn Sister

Dazzled By The Light

The Halloween Incident

See You Smile (Love's Landscapes)

Merry F***cking Christmas

Eagle Man and Mr Hawk (Love is an Open Road)

Not a Word (Love is an Open Road)

Locked in the Moment (Love Unlocked)

A Springful of Winters (Seasons of Love)

Beaten Track Publishing

For more titles from Beaten Track Publishing,
please visit our website:

http://www.beatentrackpublishing.com

Thanks for reading!